T0343648

THE WOMAN IN VALENCIA

Annie Perreault

THE WOMAN
IN VALENCIA

Translated from the French by Ann Marie Boulanger

QC FICTION

Revision: Peter McCambridge
Proofreading: David Warriner, Elizabeth West
Book design: Folio infographie
Cover & logo: Maison 1608 by Solisco
Cover art: *Spirit Level* by Jordan Sullivan, jordan-sullivan.com
Fiction editor: Peter McCambridge

Copyright © 2018 Les Éditions Alto
Originally published under the title *La femme de Valence*
by Les Éditions Alto, 2018 (Québec City, Québec)
Translation copyright © Ann Marie Boulanger

ISBN 978-1-77186-237-0 pbk; 978-1-77186-238-7 epub; 978-1-77186-239-4 pdf

Legal Deposit, 1st quarter 2021
Bibliothèque et Archives nationales du Québec
Library and Archives Canada

Published by QC Fiction, an imprint of Baraka Books
Printed and bound in Québec

Trade Distribution & Returns
Canada - UTP Distribution: UTPdistribution.com
United States & World - Independent Publishers Group: IPGbook.com

We acknowledge the financial support for translation and promotion of the Société de développement des entreprises culturelles (SODEC), the Government of Québec tax credit for book publishing administered by SODEC, the Government of Canada, and the Canada Council for the Arts.

*"Indifference is the paralysis of the soul;
it is premature death."*

— Anton Chekhov, "A Boring Story"
(translated by Richard Pevear and Larissa Volokhonsky)

*"How to avoid going back? Get lost. I don't know how.
You'll learn. I need some signpost to lead me astray.
Make your mind a blank. Refuse to recognize familiar
landmarks. Turn your steps towards the most hostile
point on the horizon, towards the vast marshlands,
bewilderingly criss-crossed by a thousand causeways."*

— Marguerite Duras, *The Vice-Consul*
(translated by Eileen Ellenbogen)

A terrible chill runs through your body when you think back to Valencia.

And yet, it was August in a city by the sea, almost the end of summer vacation, the tail end of a suffocatingly hot summer. It happened next to the pool, when the light was at its peak.

You were stretched out in what little shade there was to be had on a rooftop, your mind elsewhere. Not one for swanky hotels and bikinis, you were wearing a suit that you'd bought the day before, strings knotted tightly over your hipbones and around your neck. You were lazing on a deck chair, an open book resting on your stomach like a delicate paper tent. You had absolutely no expectations, other than soaking up the sun, getting a little rest, lazing in the tropical heat. Lying there limply, you were completely worry free, untroubled by any thoughts of the past, wanting nothing other than to be left alone. Through heavy eyelids, your gaze travelled idly between the sky, the perfectly straight row of empty lounge chairs, and the smattering of moles on your thigh like tiny black pinheads embedded in your flesh.

You must've spent a good hour lounging like that, killing time, when you noticed something moving out of the corner of your eye, to your left. A woman was walking toward you. You turned to look over your shoulder and at that precise second, Valencia became—and would forever remain—a city of ice. The sky turned to grey, to concrete.

You were the last person to speak to her. On the roof of the Valencia Palace Hotel, you did nothing to stop the withered blonde woman. You didn't lay a hand on her shoulder, didn't suggest that she sit or lie down, didn't offer her a glass of water. You didn't even light her cigarette when she fumbled with her lighter, wrist trembling as the blood dripped slowly from the large white dressing, which you stared at like it was the most ordinary thing in the world—a sweatband or a Band-Aid on an insect bite. You didn't come up with the right thing to say, the right thing to do, the right way to look at her. A loving mother though you were, a considerate person whose heart was normally in the right place, at that moment, you were completely unmoved. Uncaring. You were pure ice. An indifferent witness to the stranger's distress, watching the events unfold in an inexplicable fog.

It's that fog that you returned to Spain to try to dispel, alone, six years after the fact. You booked a plane ticket to Barcelona, a train ticket to Valencia, and a room for three nights at the Valencia Palace Hotel.

And now, here I am in Valencia, retracing your steps.

I

THREE DAYS IN VALENCIA
(The arbitrary colour of the sky)

THE WOMAN IN VALENCIA

That day, like every other day, the fish had glided back and forth overhead. With their necks craned backward and their mouths gaped open, the thousands of visitors to the Oceanogràfic aquarium had stood for an eternity watching them through the walls of a glass tunnel.

For Claire Halde and the other tourists, the memory of these wriggling fish would eventually fade. So would the mental images of the orca and dolphin shows, despite the applause they'd earned. The penguinarium and its gentoos would also be forgotten, like the names and faces of so many of the people who come and go in our lives: classmates, neighbours, teachers, colleagues, one-night stands, travel companions.

Most of the carefree schoolmates whose hands Claire had held in the schoolyard as a child, the smiles of the old ladies she'd greeted politely on the sidewalk, the voices of the many teachers who'd spent a hundred and eighty days a year screeching chalk across the blackboard, the bored co-workers she'd sat next to, pecking away at a yellowed QWERTY keyboard to pay for her tuition, and even some of the men she'd kissed hungrily in the dead of night: All will end up evaporating from her thoughts.

But Claire Halde will never forget the woman in Valencia, the strange blonde who'd approached her that afternoon by the pool at the Valencia Palace Hotel. Claire clings stubbornly to her memory—her skin, face, voice, hair, expression—even though they'd co-existed for all of ten minutes, the time it had taken to exchange five sentences, to stare at one another in silence. Claire had never introduced herself or so much as asked the woman her name. She will forever remain "the woman in Valencia," a fleeting ghost.

———

The woman's skin tells the story of her life, a tale spun from the tremors that run through her body in places. The story, one of profound despair, is written plainly on her forehead, in deep horizontal lines that arch down to meet the ends of her eyebrows. The anguish is inscribed in the corners of her mouth, furrows cultivated by bitterness, fine lines etched by roughness and worry. Her flesh sags in places where more comfortable circumstances make for skin that is firmer and healthier, scrupulously cleansed and moisturized daily in front of gleaming mirrors, at spotless vanities. There's never really anything alarming to be found on the surfaces disinfected and polished by foreign cleaning ladies, who pick up little pots of cream and shaving accessories without resentment. These bright, spacious bathrooms are worlds away from the sinks that reek of mildew, caulking eroded by colonies of black pinpricks that look like gnats, surrounded by cracked, peeling tiles splattered with blood, semen, urine and shit that no one ever bothers to clean. For the woman from the pool, in Valencia, sinks like these are par for the course: rust-streaked porcelain, bright orange stains blossoming from wet razors left lying on the counter. All that filth turns her stomach as she bends over to splash water on her face, pick her teeth with a fingernail, stare at herself in the mirror and assess the damage.

———

The woman makes her way toward the pool. First in a straight line, hips swaying in her skintight pencil skirt, long, gangly legs propelling her forward in fits and starts, then in a zigzagging pattern around the patio furniture. She looks like she's searching for a particular spot, or a particular someone; her intention isn't quite clear. The stiff fabric of her steel-grey skirt, a perma-press polyester vise gleaming in the sun, compresses her body into dejected folds. Against the bright sunlight, her silhouette is shockingly frail and bony. There's tension in her hips, a tightness to her jaw. She's wearing rather conservative heels and a tasteful blouse that's partially unbuttoned, revealing a hint of waxy-looking skin underneath. Her hair is a faded blonde. At first glance, she looks like she might be foreign, Eastern European maybe. On her face, there's a look of profound melancholy, and her eyes are bleak and lifeless. Her arms hang limply, and a large leather purse hooked over her wrist swings back and forth in the void, in time with her advancing steps.

A trick of the eye makes the purse appear disproportionately heavy and awkward. The mauve tote bag, neither shiny nor matte, is broken in as only leather and hides can be after a certain amount of time. Aged and cracked, worn and dull, dried out in the creases—a fair representation of the woman herself. The woman who is now advancing on Claire Halde across the roof of the Valencia Palace Hotel.

———

In a corner set back slightly from the pool, a couple of vacationers are stretched out on fully extended lounge chairs, heads lolling, feet splayed out, bellies slack under layers of fat and skin bronzing in the sun. They could be dozing or simply daydreaming behind their dark glasses. They could be mannequins in a shop window.

Claire watches her children float like starfish with their father in the pool. They're having a ball. Jean was right: An afternoon swim is doing them good. It's precisely the kind of treat they enjoy on holiday, but it wasn't exactly how she'd pictured her trip to Valencia, forfeiting the charming streets of the Old Town, sacrificing an ocean view—all for a pool. And now the woman with the dead eyes has appeared and she's speaking to Claire in a foreign language she doesn't recognize. Claire answers her in Spanish, then in English, but she's having trouble understanding her; the woman's voice is hoarse, garbled, confused.

"Can you help me? My bag, take my bag."

The woman puts the purse down at her feet, revealing a square of gauze taped over the veins on her right wrist.

The dressing is white and carefully applied, like a nurse would do. Claire casts a sidelong glance at the pristine square covering the woman's injury and her throat contracts.

Blood is trickling from either side of the folded piece of white cotton, running in red rivulets down her alarmingly pale arm. The stranger ignores it, caught up in trying to unzip her bag. Her hands are shaking, and her movements are clumsy. Claire looks away, back to the pool and her children. She feels numb and everything sounds muffled, as though someone were holding her head underwater, blocking out all the noise on the surface. The flow of oxygen to her brain has slowed to a crawl. Claire has never seen anyone bleeding like that, from a self-inflicted wound. But she's seen the scars before, once on a man at a party and another time on a young woman she'd worked with as a camp counsellor. Claire no longer remembers the names of these people who'd discreetly shown her the inside of their wrist, like a shared secret. Time had marched on over their skin. The cuts had closed, healed, faded.

It dawns on Claire that the woman must've just come from a doctor's office or been discharged from the psychiatric ward of a nearby hospital. But the blood is still flowing, streaming from her wrist onto her palm and down her fingers.

Her eyes riveted to the dressing, Claire asks the woman if she needs help, suggests they call someone, summon an ambulance, drive her to a clinic. This seems to spook the woman.

"No, no, no, no! No help, just the bag."

Claire backs off. She considers the possibility that the woman might be in the country illegally, that she has her reasons for not wanting to involve the authorities, just as she has her reasons for trying to take her life. The blood continues to run down the woman's wrist, but she pays it no attention, rummaging frantically through her purse. Claire is seized with fright, imagining a gun, a knife, her children witnessing what's about to happen. She's paralyzed by the force of the premonition: This woman is going to shoot herself in the head, right here in front of me, in front of my son and daughter. The scenario is immediately replaced by the thought of the woman pulling a knife from her bag and threatening to slash Claire's throat with it.

Then, nothing. In Claire's mind, thoughts and fears mingle with silence, then turn to hunks of glass and metal that collide, cracking and shattering into pieces.

Time seems to be splintering in slow motion, like when someone drowns or a ship flounders in a storm. At that moment, nothing else exists but the purse, a gaping black hole that's swallowing up the rooftop terrace, the pool, the kids floating like starfish on the water's surface, the Valencian sky, the fifteen floors of the Valencia Palace, the lounge chair that Claire shrinks even further into.

Finally, the woman pulls out a pack of Lucky Strikes. She offers one to Claire, who waves it away. With trembling fingers, the stranger lights a cigarette. She hands her bag to Claire and moves to a corner of the terrace to smoke. Claire sets the bag down on the end of her chaise longue and eyes it nervously, as though a rat might suddenly crawl out of it. She inspects a cut on her finger and checks her hands for blood.

Claire doesn't immediately grasp what's happening. She watches her children playing in the pool. They're laughing, clinging to their dad's neck, splashing each other. They're happy.

She can't have them see what's going on with this woman. All her attention is focused on them: Protect the children, don't scare the children.

The woman smokes for a minute next to the bushes, looks down at the ground nervously, and skirts the greenery along the edge of the rooftop like she's looking for something. Then she shuffles back to Claire, who tries to hand the bag back to her.

"Keep the bag, keep the bag!"

Her tone is harsh, annoyed. She mutters something, a question that Claire doesn't catch. She becomes agitated and she's having trouble forming her words. Claire thrusts her beach towel at the woman and points her toward a blue door to the right of the pool. The stranger staggers off in the direction of the ladies' changing room, mopping up the blood on her arm as she goes.

Perched on the edge of her deck chair, Claire can almost feel her nerves thrumming. She tries to get Jean's attention—surely he'll recognize the fear in her eyes or notice the look of panic on her face. She wants to call out to him for help, but she's gone mute. The danger is setting off alarm bells inside her. Her body is firing off a series of signals that are coursing through her: nerve impulses, a surge of adrenaline, a quickening of her heartbeat, sudden dry mouth, waves of nausea. Primal instincts kick in. Her brain is foggy, and she's tensed like an animal ready to pounce. The balance between Claire Halde's sympathetic and parasympathetic nervous systems is about to give way.

She remains there, motionless, petrified, the purse resting against her bare thigh, watching the closed door of the ladies' room. It's midnight blue and scuffed up near the bottom, and Claire has no idea what she'll see when it finally swings open, but then it does, and the woman emerges.

A blonde bag of bones, those are the words that come to mind when Claire sees the woman in Valencia once again making her way across the patio. *Skin*, too, *waxy, grey skin.* Narrow hips, a tight, flat stomach, scrawny arms, a sinewy neck that's nothing but skin and bones propping up a head of washed-out blonde hair. The look in her eyes is dark and empty, devoid of all light. Her body moves jerkily, like a marionette with invisible strings that are holding up her head and controlling her arms and legs, which carry her to the edge of the roof and over the railing in a scissor-like motion. She crouches down and rests her bottom on the ledge for a moment—a few seconds or a few minutes, who can say, time seems to stand still—and then the woman gently eases herself into the void.

On the boulevard far below, passersby scream.

———

Presumably, the body—under the combined effects of adrenaline and helplessness, overcome by disgust and impotence, filled with dismay and anger—might simply give out: dizziness, a sudden drop in blood pressure, retching, disorientation due to emotional shock, or even a momentary loss of speech, which can happen sometimes.

Some people's teeth chatter, others start to shake uncontrollably, like they've just emerged bone dry from freezing cold water. Others experience an emotional short circuit, flipping the switch on pain—theirs and others'—numbing themselves to their feelings as a means of self-preservation.

The shock can sometimes be followed by night terrors, mystery rashes—the skin talks, after all—or clumps of hair falling out in handfuls to block the bathtub drain, floating in the soup like dead flies. No one is immune to sudden baldness, the kind that leaves the scalp riddled with unsightly and glaringly obvious bare patches. And yet, nothing. None of this happened.

———

Claire strides purposefully toward the crowd gathered near the ambulance. She says what she has to say without hesitating. She states her version of the facts in carefully enunciated Spanish.

Her skin most likely gives her away. She doesn't realize it (and won't until the next time she looks in a mirror), but she's deathly pale. There's a horrible pasty taste in her mouth, her heart is racing, and a mental fog is creeping in, clouding the scene and blocking out any immediate thoughts.

She's on autopilot: calm and collected, saying all the right things, leg muscles tensed for action. She's rock steady on her feet, which is hard to believe for someone who's fainted more than half a dozen times since her teens. The first time, she blacked out suddenly on the scorching sand, beach chair folded under her arm, after reading *Anna Karenina* in the sun for hours. Then, when she was fifteen, in a case of history repeating itself, she passed out in a heap of smarting skin after exiting a tanning booth, naked and cocky. Next came the time, in her early twenties, when a stranger's arms were the only thing that prevented her pale, limp body from hitting the floor of a crowded metro car during rush hour on the blue line. Years later, she was introduced to the term "vasovagal syncope" for the first time when, bare-assed on a paper sheet with a speculum between her legs, she emerged from a fog after a ham-handed doctor perforated her uterus with a copper IUD. Over the years, she'd come to dread what might happen if she stood up too quickly; she shrunk from heatwaves and developed an aversion to large crowds. But all the precautions in the world didn't keep her from keeling over at a rave, dehydrated and fresh off a heartbreak, or from swooning after getting out of bed moments after having her second baby. Another time after that, she slumped to the cold, beige tiled floor of a suburban shopping mall after donating blood to the Red Cross. And as if that wasn't enough, she managed to faint dead away in a snowbank, wrapped in a bubble gum-pink bathrobe, after stepping out of an overheated sauna in the middle of the Ural Mountains, the same place where a ten-ton meteor would blast across the sky a few years later. And, most recently, as her terrified kids pawed through the medicine cabinet in search of a Band-Aid for their mother, she dropped like a sack of potatoes after slicing her thumb open with a bread knife. And yet, despite this ridiculous propensity to fainting and her sensitive vagal nerve, she remains steadfastly upright on the sidewalk in front of the Valencia Palace Hotel.

She stands frozen to the spot, her eyes glued to a chunk of heel bone that someone really should do something about.

MONTREAL, SUMMER 2009

Head under the sink, Claire gingerly picks up mouldy bits of old sponges, stiff and crumbling, wondering disgustedly why she even kept them in the first place. The same disdain is levelled at gnarled, rusty balls of steel wool, stained rags and the dregs of a bottle of Windex. Claire Halde scrubs or tosses anything that looks remotely sketchy.

She checks her watch and sighs. Air France flight 347 for Barcelona is scheduled for takeoff at 7:45 p.m. Tonight, another family will move into their house for the summer. Catalan strangers will sleep in their beds, shit in their toilet, stand their toothbrushes up in the ceramic cup that Claire has soaked in bleach overnight to dissolve weeks of slimy stains and fine lines of black mould built up in the cracks.

Jean is gathering up all the electronics—cables and chargers, batteries and cases, Bluetooth accessories and adaptors—which he's organizing obsessively in a large bag full of pouches and compartments as though he were packing survival gear for a perilous Antarctic expedition.

Noticing Claire ass-up furiously scrubbing the insides of their kitchen cabinets, he snaps, "Would you give it a rest? This isn't the Ritz. They must be cool if they've agreed to a house swap. They're not going to freak out over a bit of dirt under the sink."

"You don't get it," Claire retorts, letting loose great streams of Fantastik in an attempt to erase months of cutting corners in their weekly cleaning routine. "I don't want them seeing any trace of us and our lazy-ass habits. It's bad enough I saw a centipede last night."

"A what?"

The night before, she'd scrubbed the bathtub with so much elbow grease and Ajax that tiny cracks had opened up across the knuckles of her index fingers. A thin crust of blood had formed around the edges of the deepest cut. Her dry, rough skin still smarted from the harsh cleaning products. Before going to bed, with an aching shoulder but a deep sense of satisfaction at the newly gleaming porcelain, she'd run herself a steaming hot bath, which she'd sunk into, her thoughts spinning with everything she still had to do before they left. Between the ammonia fumes still lingering in the air and the clouds of steam building up in the bathroom, Claire had had trouble breathing. Relaxing her neck and shoulder muscles, she'd let herself slide deeper into the tub until she could feel the water lapping at the hair at the back of her neck. She'd closed her eyes but couldn't relax. The heat wasn't agreeing with her; her heart had begun to quiver strangely—a harmless cardiac episode, but worrying, nonetheless. She'd never liked taking baths. She'd straightened up like a shot when she spotted an ugly bug scurrying between the faucets and up the wall, its yellow carapace gyrating back and forth.

"A centipede! You know? A house centipede."

She mimes the insect's creepy-crawly legs with her fingers.

"Like a millipede, but uglier—a hairy millipede. Think I should've killed it? It was moving really fast and skittering all over the place. God knows where it went."

Jean has never heard of centipedes and has a suitcase to zip up. Claire goes to their room, pulls all their clothes out of their drawers and stuffs them into big garbage bags, which she shoves in the kids' closet. On their dresser, next to a mushroom lamp with a white polka-dotted red cap and a Lego armoured vehicle, a fish is wriggling in its bowl, on the surface of the water. Claire walks over to toss in a few flakes of fish food.

"Kids, kids, come see this! Quick! Your fish has a..."

Claire lifts her son up so he can get a better look at the fishbowl.

"Balou has a new friend. A centipede. A house centipede!"

But the centipede is just lying there, motionless in the bowl, plastered to the glass, head down in a perfectly straight line. Its body looks bloated.

"Is it dangerous?" her daughter asks.

"I don't know. Anyways, it's dead."

Claire picks up the fishbowl and carries it to the bathroom. With a net, she gingerly scoops out the tangled mass of legs, shakes the corpse out into the toilet and flushes. The fish begins to twitch nervously, seized with convulsions that quickly peak, then goes completely still. Claire taps the thick glass with her finger. The fish doesn't react. She rocks the bowl gently. The water ripples, but the fish remains motionless, belly up in the water.

"Jean..."

Claire walks over to her husband, holding the fishbowl in her hands.

"Maybe he had a heart attack. Or the centipede poisoned him. Or maybe it was a panic attack."

"Shit! He could've picked a better time. We'd better not tell the kids," Jean sighs wearily. "We'll deal with it when we get home."

Claire dumps the water and the fish into the toilet bowl, with the same coldness with which she'll one day say, in a single breath, Jean, I don't love you anymore. Go on, get out of here. She pulls the chain. Balou disappears into the sewers in concentric circles. She stows the empty bowl, the pouch of fish flakes and the net under the immaculate kitchen sink. She takes a moment to rip up the note she'd written in Spanish explaining to their guests how to feed the fish and clean the tank.

At the last second, she grabs her travel journals in a panic from her nightstand and stashes them in a shoebox, which she hides behind a pile of blankets in the linen closet, only to promptly forget where she put them. Once home from their vacation, they will search high and low for that bloody shoebox full of Japanese notebooks with the tan covers, like a collection of bleak Soviet-era packages. Years of handwritten confidences, line after line of her life story recorded in a rainbow of inks and leads, a stream of cursive writing, frenetic and illegible in places, that will only be found a few years later when they are packing up to move—but let's not get ahead of ourselves. The taxi has just pulled up, and chaos and confusion break out in an attempt to get people and possessions loaded and ready to go: two kids, two suitcases, one stroller, one blankie, and one carry-on backpack.

Four passports? Check, confirms Claire Halde as she pulls the zipper closed on her purse. She closes her eyes, takes a few deep breaths, releases the tension from her jaw, and takes one last look back at their house. All is well.

"To the airport, please."

Let the vacation begin.

BARCELONA

As they leave for Spain, they have no idea how their summer will unfold. They have five weeks of vacation and the keys to an apartment in the Sant Antoni district of Barcelona. They have no set plans for their summer in Catalonia, apart from taking things hour by hour, day by day, and wandering wherever their next adventure takes them. Time passes in a succession of days, then weeks, peaceful and quiet: museum trips and meals taken on the patio, all-you-can-eat *patatas bravas* and *churros* for the kids, afternoons at the beach, *cava* and *tinto de verano*, miles of late-night runs for Claire and Jean, each one in turn, and masses of Iberian ham. The nights all meld into one, indistinguishable. They barely make love, but the act has become so mechanical that it doesn't even register with Claire anymore. When she thinks back on it, Claire Halde can't picture herself climaxing between those sheets, in that unremarkable room. She seems to recall a flowered bedspread and white furniture. There were French doors that opened up onto the patio, but she's forgotten what the sunlight looked like in the morning, when the first light of dawn would filter into the room and she'd open her eyes with indifference at the prospect of another day spent playing tourist.

LEAVING BARCELONA

That July, not a single drop of rain falls on Barcelona. Since they're not in the habit of spending their summers in the Catalonian capital, they don't notice anything out of the ordinary at first. Seasonal temperatures, they tell themselves. But it doesn't take long before Claire and Jean are wilting under the blazing sun, seeking out shade at every opportunity.

The mounting string of days without rain becomes the reason for everything that disappoints, disorients and discourages them: their exhaustion, their lovers' quarrels that are a sign of things to come, the shops and museums closed for the annual summer holiday, their lack of enthusiasm for planning outings, the price of vegetables, the blandness of the strawberries. In a way, it's even why they end up in Valencia—the need to get away from the stifling heat of Barcelona, if only for three days.

Their little side trip gets off to a bad start. It's the first week of August, and the car rental places have nothing left but stick shifts. They look at each other sheepishly, embarrassed that neither of them knows how to drive one. As they leave the rental agency, to get a laugh out of Claire, Jean hums, "I'm a loser baby, so why don't you kill me?"

So, they book four train tickets to Valencia departing from Barcelona Sants.

AT THE TRAIN STATION

Claire Halde and her family leave Barcelona at 9:44 a.m. from platform 12, destination Valencia. She has no way of knowing that she'll make almost the same trip again six years later, only alone. At the moment, she's pushing a toddler in a striped romper, leading a little girl by the hand, rushing a man who doesn't like to be rushed. The purse slung across her chest is banging into her hip and digging into her belly uncomfortably as she makes her way across the concourse. She's sweating and she has the look of a harried mom who desperately wants to be on time but fully expects to be sidetracked by last-minute pee emergencies, squabbling kids and distracted husbands: Honey, have you seen my passport? She leads her crew single file across the uneven concrete like a toy sailboat cutting a course through the glassy waters of a park pond.

ON THE TRAIN

Outside the train window, the countryside flashes by in an endless, unremarkable blur, a monochromatic sea of yellow. Buildings are few and far between, and the light is pooling spectacularly in the furrows of the barren fields. Some of the passengers are staring at the passing landscape with waning attention, losing the battle with sleep. Others, riveted to their mobiles, engrossed in work or a book, don't even look up at the stunning scenery and coastline.

Claire resists sleep. The view soothes her, and her eyes linger on the landscape. Her eyelids are drooping; her son's head is resting in her lap, hair damp at the back of his neck. The train seems to cleave the earth, moving forward over the miles and hours in a numbing rolling motion. All sense of time and space disappear, and the line blurs between inside and outside. The train follows the tracks—all that steel, assembled by men from another century who toiled hungrily for countless hours under the fierce sun so that she, Claire Halde, soon to be thirty-four, should find herself here on this summer day, in second class, compartment 7, comfortably ensconced in a navy blue upholstered window seat with hygienic headrest cover, headed to Valencia for a few days' stay at a hotel.

DISCOVERING VALENCIA

Valencia: citrus groves, the coastline, neither north nor south, but somewhere in the middle of Spain's east coast, in the centre of the *horta*. Claire Halde had only a vague notion of the geography and she'd had to look it up on a map at one point. Or maybe it's the high school Spanish classes coming back to her, particularly the lesson on train stations and train travel: *¿ A qué hora sale el tren por Bilbao por favor ?* She remembers the stern voice of the man on the recording who'd repeat each sentence twice, followed by the sudden, loud click of the teacher pressing the tape recorder button. She recalls the problems she'd had wrapping her lips and tongue around the *jota*, hesitating over the tonic accent, stumbling over the guttural sounds and cursing the Castilian letters *g*, *j*, and *r*—consonants and syllables that thumbed their noses at her and seemed to clatter clumsily against her teeth, wet with saliva, when they should have bounced suavely off her palate and sprung

35

forth with agility and confidence from her vibrating vocal cords. She remembers feeling like she'd swallowed the sounds rather than spit them out (without the spit, of course). With jaw tired and aching and feeling like a marble-mouth, she'd longed for silence, hiding behind an insipid smile and the intense and mysterious gaze of a precocious teenager, as much as to say, why waste my breath, leaving people wondering whether she was stuck-up or just shy.

Valencia: sounds, voices on a cassette in Spanish class, and oranges. That's about it. No music, no visuals. The foggy notion of a paella and a vowel-heavy adjective that rolls off the tongue: Valencian. Nothing specific in the way of architecture except for a few impressive examples of Gothic structures, which don't particularly interest Claire Halde. None of the originality of Gaudí in Barcelona or the appeal of the museums in Madrid, no Goya or Velasquez to contemplate during never-ending museum visits, no trace of Picasso, none of the mysterious charm of the Moorish buildings of Andalusia, not even any real mountains to speak of—you have to go north for those, to the Pyrenees, another elegantly written word, with all those *e*'s and that *y*. The mystics and the trekkers won't find any pilgrimages here; the city doesn't have much in the way of attractions, or at least that's what the tour guides used to say, but that's changing now at the turn of the century, with the City of Arts and Sciences springing up at the mouth of the old Turia riverbed, a daring architectural feat, all fish and ocean floors, glass and waterlily-inspired roofs, and a seventy-five-ton steel eyelid. Alright, time to explore Valencia.

STAYING IN VALENCIA:
THE VALENCIA PALACE HOTEL

A taxi drops Claire Halde and her family off in front of the Valencia Palace Hotel. Claire pays the fare while Jean hoists the suitcases out of the trunk. The children wait obediently as their luggage is piled up on the sidewalk. The lobby is bright, with windows on two sides, one of which overlooks the congress centre designed by Sir Norman Foster, where there seems to be absolutely nothing going on; the deserted building appears almost frozen in time, snuffed out in the Valencian summer. Dead leaves rustle on the ground in front of the glass entrance. The fountains are dry.

At fifteen storeys high, the towering Valencia Palace casts a shadow over the building next door. It's like a giant cruise ship run aground in the middle of the city, in the middle of nowhere, its triangular prow bearing down on Avinguda de las Cortes Valencianas.

They'd chosen it for the pool, for the four stars, to make the kids happy. Even though they'd known it wasn't in the best of locations, they'd given in to the temptation of a summer deal. They couldn't have predicted that their bargain trip would become a catalyst in the demise of their relationship.

At the front desk, they're given a key card for room 714, where they set down their bags. Claire's first impression is that the decor is cold and impersonal.

She remarks to Jean that they could be in any city, anywhere in the world. The windows don't open; there's no whiff of city air, no warmth, no noise. And they're nowhere near the sea.

The room is dark and gloomy. The thick, heavy, floral-patterned curtains will stay drawn for most of their visit. Claire and Jean look out the window at everything happening below: cars driving through the roundabout, taxis pulling up, doors opening and closing, smoke rising from a distant chimney, and a Leroy Merlin warehouse store, rectangular and white, sitting next to a highway. They won't touch the curtains again after that, because nothing about their immediate surroundings, about the drab, boring Valencia outside their window, holds any interest for them.

The pool is on the fourth floor, on a rooftop terrace tucked into the shadow of the looming hotel with the square windows. There's a sign on the wall: No Lifeguard on Duty. Further along, there's a line of potted plants and leafy green hedges that pass for a natural privacy screen, a few spindly trees chosen for their wind resistance and, in the way of furniture, deck chairs— mostly empty—lined up along the edge of the pool.

There's little shade to be found around the pool. The afternoon sun makes you screw up your face and squint your eyes and turns sensitive skin a delicate shade of pink on the tips of noses, foreheads, bare shoulders and tiny toes. The city below is invisible from the rooftop terrace of the Valencia Palace Hotel, giving the impression that the terrace itself is propped up in the sky, suspended high above Valencia.

If they'd been on a romantic getaway, they would have probably booked less extravagant accommodations, like a B&B or a quaint hotel in the Old Town. The furniture would have been dark wood, worn to a sheen and scuffed in places, and the bedsprings might have squeaked. The windows would have opened onto the street and the curtains been faded in the folds. The smells and sounds of the city would have permeated the room. Valencia would have seemed less cold.

GETTING AROUND VALENCIA

They end up isolated from the touristy part of Valencia, in the mostly forgotten and out-of-the-way neighbourhood of Beniferri, between the Old Town and the business district, north of Campanar, which they visit by subway, bus and tram. They consult their colourful tourist maps, but there are absolutely no points of interest to speak of; they stare indifferently out the windows at the succession of nondescript streets rolling by.

Early in the evening, after a dip in the pool, they head out to explore Ciutat Vella, promising the kids that if they don't act up or argue on the bus, they'll take them to the Horchatería Santa Catalina to dunk *fartons* in *horchata*. They cram onto the N3 bus, breathing in the rank smell of the other passengers' sweat after a day of work, their citrusy perfumes lingering at the napes of their necks and in their hair, and the fresh scent of toddlers squirming in the aisle and on the moulded plastic seats.

DAY 2 ITINERARY: THE MAIN ATTRACTIONS

The next day, Claire, Jean and the children slip on sundresses and breezy shorts. Feet shod in strappy sandals, they set out on their itinerary for day 2: the City of Arts and Sciences in the morning for an exhausting visit to the Oceanogràfic, a quick lunch in the port district, followed by a mid-afternoon stroll by the seaside.

They take their time at the aquarium, admiring the countless fish swimming behind the glass. They do their best to catch a glimmer in the beady eyes set among the scales, to lock watery gazes with the tiny black marbles embedded in the wriggling bodies. But, each time, the fish switch directions as one, darting off to the side or hiding among the seaweed. They're both fascinated and awed by the unpredictability of the schools of fish and their slow-motion synchronized swimming, their impeccably choreographed moves, like flocks of birds. Every now and then, a big fish breaks ranks and swims toward the glass, and the children get all excited, only for it to do an about-face at the last second. It's almost like a game, a planned fake-out designed to get a rise out of the visitors and make them think they're actually communing with the sea creatures. The children spend a few minutes searching vainly for Balou's distant cousins among the smaller fish.

They line up for the dolphin show and "ooh" and "ahh" at the animals' prowess. They marvel at the glow of the jellyfish and their languorous underwater movements, before deciding they've had enough of all the scales, tropical colours and quivering gills. After a few halfhearted attempts at building sandcastles, they stroll through the pedestrian-only streets until they come across a charming café, where they drop into the aluminum chairs on the patio for a drink. For a short while, they munch on peanuts and mouth-puckeringly salty olives, rolling the pits around under their tongues, before heading back to the hotel where everyone can't wait to jump in the pool.

WE MIGHT AS WELL FLY

The woman in Valencia leaves a trail of blood behind her as she walks, a line of bright red dots on the wooden deck.

She's standing at the edge of the roof, relieved of her purse, one wrist sliced open. The powdery taste of the pills lingers in her mouth, burning her throat as they make their way slowly through her insides: One dose, two doses, nine doses penetrate the walls of her stomach and seep into her blood, gumming up her tongue and clouding her brain, short-circuiting her nervous system, turning her arms to mush, and setting her legs, lips and bony fingers trembling.

She lowers herself onto the ledge, legs dangling over the side, vein pulsing, body riddled with poison, no rope to hang herself with, overcome by the need to end it all.

We might as well fly.

On impulse, she lifts her bottom, her death wish now an obsession. She spreads her arms open wide, reflexively, like a newborn baby who's just been set down.

She's hoping for a dizzying fall, enough of a vertical drop to kill herself, enough sky to imagine herself gliding, gliding, gliding like a paper airplane, to experience weightlessness for a few seconds. All she wants is a few feet of freedom before hitting the concrete, like a breakaway in a cycling race, that thrilling feeling of slicing through the air.

In the land of the living, to take to the air—to be everything that lives and flies, for once to be everything you've always wanted to be, to assume the shape of every creature whose acts of flight you've ever watched in amazement: a hummingbird suspended in midair, a falcon soaring on the wind, a butterfly and a firefly, a dragonfly skimming the surface of the water, a ladybug rising from the palm of a child's hand, a bumblebee filled with nectar hovering over a patch of flowers, a snow goose or a Siberian crane set resolutely on its course, a great blue heron, a tiny chickadee, a gannet, a swarm of insects, a flock of geese, a flying squirrel, or even a flying fish, leaping above the horizon, its fins glimmering brilliantly against a slice of blue amid a shower of light, its body writhing in the air, between sea and sky, suspended, floating, but for gravity.

Before hitting the concrete, to know what it felt like to fall through the air; then, from head to toe, to suddenly and completely shatter, and with a wet thud, to die.

———

It's both easy and excruciating to imagine a body falling through the void. Something just doesn't compute; the brain has a hard time seeing the action through to the end, picturing the violent impact with the ground.

Falling from a height is an extremely common dream. We've all felt that dizzying sensation, that stomach-churning feeling of the midnight free-fall and the terror of jolting awake just before hitting the ground, as the brain slips back into the driver's seat, the eyes fly open, and the fall is interrupted just in time. In our imagined scenarios of someone falling or intentionally jumping from a height, the body rarely hits the ground; it stays suspended. In dreams and movies, there's never an impact.

We can all picture scenes from action movies or old war footage of soldiers rocketing through the sky, spread-eagled, the instant before their parachute deploys. We also remember the morning of September 11, 2001. Claire had been sitting on the edge of the unmade bed, her thigh pressed up against Jean's (that was before the kids were born), in a dingy postage stamp of an apartment with perma-stained linoleum. Like everyone else that day, she'd stayed glued to the TV, transfixed by the images of the people throwing themselves out the windows of the World Trade Center. *We have jumpers*, one commentator had said.

It's hard to forget *The Falling Man*, that iconic photo of the man, body perfectly vertical, one knee bent, falling head-first against the backdrop of the New York City skyscraper. There are no signs of flames or of the tragedy playing out several floors above; only a perfectly framed slice of architectural purity, a canvas of clean, dark lines captured just moments before the building collapsed, a silhouette suspended in the act of dying, of choosing his death. *We might as well fly*, is what might have crossed his mind as he made the final decision of his life.

Claire doesn't see the body of the woman in Valencia slice through the few square feet of air that separate the roof from the sidewalk. She sees the gleam in her eyes ten seconds before she goes through with the act and the subtle forward motion of her body, and in the time it takes to blink once, she imagines the rest: the fall and the impact, the bones and the concrete.

Because she didn't see it happen, there's nothing realistic about the fall that she forces herself to picture over and over; it resists all attempts at reconstruction. When Claire thinks back on the scene, it's not a real body that she sees plunging four floors in the space of just a few seconds. Instead, her memory conjures up images of crash test dummies. It's a ragdoll, a fake body without bones or blood that Claire pictures flying through the air when she thinks about the woman in Valencia's fall. A naked jumping jack, head round like an egg, with empty eye sockets staring out of a featureless face.

Then there are the famous photos of bodies sprawled out on the ground after "the most beautiful suicide." It's hard not to cringe at the thought of a fatal fall. Instinctively, we turn our head, squeeze our eyes shut. Yet we can't help but gaze with fascination on the luminous beauty of Evelyn McHale after her leap from the eighty-sixth floor of the Empire State Building, immortalized by Warhol in his "Death and Disasters" series. What possible explanation could there be for the peaceful countenance of the young accountant, entombed in the wreckage of the car she landed on, her unblemished body resting on its bed of crushed metal, draped in the elegant folds of her red dress, legs slender and feet bare, eyelids gently closed as though she were taking a nap on Fifth Avenue?

Frozen next to her lounge chair, the oversized tote bag dangling from her wrist, Claire can't picture the brutal end of the scene. In disbelief, she replays what's just happened on fast forward. Each time, she stumbles over the fraction of a second when, almost as bizarrely as the woman had approached her from out of nowhere a few minutes earlier, she'd disappeared violently from her field of vision with one final backward glance. In that indefinable amount of time—one second or three minutes, who can say—an entire life was upended.

Claire turns her head toward her children and the worried face of her daughter, who's running in her direction. In her mind's eye—that of a panic-stricken mother—the woman's glance is superimposed by another image: her daughter running carefree toward her, then freezing, stopping dead, alarmed by what will become a childhood memory, a recollection of their trip to Spain. Later, Laure would come to understand that she had seen a woman die.

Claire will not explain anything to her six-year-old, who is staring at her with wide, dark eyes, eyebrows arched, baby-smooth brow furrowed with worry. Standing there dripping in her pink polka-dotted bikini, she asks her mother again: But why did that lady jump? Why? Why do you have that bag, Mama?

When retelling the story afterwards, Claire will come to say, "The sky was grey." She'll become fixated on the greyness of the sky, even though she could have sworn the sun had been blinding that day as the woman walked toward her.

She definitely seems to remember that they were both squinting as they stared at one another, that the harsh afternoon light had chased away all traces of shadow, heightening the contrasts between objects and bodies, like in the glaring light of an operating room. She'd been cemented to her deck chair, her brain addled—sun stupid, she's convinced. In the days that followed, she even remembers thinking about Meursault's argument in *The Stranger*, when he claims at his trial that he killed the Arab because of the sun. It's possible that the weather had turned suddenly, that the sky had clouded over and the air cooled off; in fact, it's not inconceivable that the clouds had rolled in late in the day and that the steel-grey sky, pregnant with the promise of a storm, had become an indelible part of her memory. The sun had played its part, then exited stage left, like a traitor, and Claire had begun to shiver. Or maybe she had simply imagined the grey sky, the cold and the chills.

Something freezes over in her mind when she pronounces the four syllables of *Valencia*. She flashes back to an ashen sky, an unmemorable room, a pool, an air-conditioned gym with treadmills and a long, mirrored wall that she runs in front of without breaking a sweat. Claire has forgotten the temperature of the Mediterranean; she's forgotten the train station and the Valencia Cathedral, but she remembers with clinical precision the feeling of freezing on the rooftop of the Valencia Palace Hotel as the woman walked over to her, handed her the purse, then threw herself over the edge.

Claire keeps a cool head. A blizzard rages in her veins, slowing her circulation to a crawl despite her mad dash to the elevator. It's just her and the purse in the metal cage as it makes its way down, and her heart—that four-chambered hollow organ—is pounding furiously in her chest.

Claire eyes the zipper on the tote bag, reluctant to open it before handing it over to the police. A woman's purse is a sacred vessel, a repository of memories and secrets: a brainbox, only pliable.

She thinks about her own purse. She wouldn't want a strange woman rummaging around in it, seeing the mess, pawing through all that junk: scraps of paper, keys, forgotten bank statements still in their envelopes, tattered receipts, little girl's drawings of bright yellow suns, chewing gum, cellophane-wrapped peppermints or fruit candies, Playmobil knight's helmet, tampons, crumbs from old snacks, stray raisins ground into the lining, torn movie stubs, pen caps, tubes of lipstick that may or may not have gone rancid, child's tiny sock, shredded old tissues, souvenirs kept for no particular reason, like the outdated Cape Cod tide chart, a dull pocket knife, a handful of messages from fortune cookies whose predictions never came true. Claire Halde has nothing to hide, other than the shame of the boring mess that has become her life.

Claire gazes at the worn leather, stretched out in places, and wonders whether anyone will miss the woman, whether somewhere children, a lover, a pimp or a boss is waiting for her.

Opening the zipper would no doubt solve the mystery of the stranger's identity: first and last name, address, age, nationality, height, eye colour, mother's maiden name. Perhaps that had been her last wish, which she'd conveyed by handing Claire the purse: not to die in anonymity. Or maybe it was the complete opposite: to shed her identity, to die incognito by leaving the purse behind. The numbers in the elevator light up one after another—third floor, second floor—and Claire still hasn't decided whether she should look inside the bloodstained purse.

When the elevator comes to a halt and the doors slide silently open onto the bright lobby, decked out with green plants and charcoal leatherette loveseats arranged around a patterned rug, Claire presses the square metal button embossed with the number 7. She presses so hard her fingertip turns white, like that will make the automatic doors close any faster as they come together in a perfect seal, like the stabbing motion will speed up the cables or the cabin, or make the light move quicker—first floor, second floor, third floor, where a man steps forward and asks in a British accent, Going down?, then takes a quick step backward when he notices that the arrow above the door is pointing up. Claire never once takes her eyes off the tote bag, which is cutting into her wrist, as the doors slide smoothly back into place with an abrupt whoosh. Bag resting against her hip, Claire waits for the 7 to light up before stepping out of the elevator and walking toward her room.

When Jean asks her a few hours later why she didn't go back downstairs to turn the bag over to the hotel staff, when he demands to know what came over her when she instead went back to their room, rolled the purse up in a towel and stashed it in her suitcase, she'll answer him clearly, with the cold detachment of a rehearsed speech: The woman said keep the bag; I respected her last wishes.

THREATS AND EMERGENCIES

A human body part, shredded muscles and ligaments, shiny cartilage—that's what Claire sees as she walks toward the paramedics. The fragment of heel bone, the size of a not-altogether ripe apricot, is some three feet from the body. It must have taken a bounce, like a rock in a game of hopscotch leaping along the concrete, leaving unsightly scratches on the delicate skin. It's just lying there, a repulsive piece of bone surrounded by flesh, barely bleeding, a perfect match to the foot injury. The woman is on her back, her legs twitching on the sidewalk.

Claire will carry the mental image of the shattered heel bone with her for a long time, and she'll think back on it often. In trying to imagine the pain that must have followed the impact, she'll conjure up the collision between bone and concrete a thousand times in the weeks to come. She'll even look it up: There are more than seven thousand nerve endings in a single foot.

She will relive the fall in her head. It would start with feeling like you'd been slammed in the stomach with a brick or an iron bar as you plummet through the void, like a punch in the gut that cleaves you in two.

Claire is familiar with that winded feeling: When she was ten, she'd fallen several feet while trying to nail a board into her new treehouse. In the blink of an eye, she'd toppled out of the tree, hammer in hand. She can still remember the pain of the bark scraping against the tender skin of her pale belly and the angry red streaks left behind. She'd lain on the ground, the wind completely knocked out of her for a few seconds, embarrassed by her clumsiness, blood in her mouth and pine needles matted in her hair.

But right now, Claire Halde is breathing freely, standing upright, trying to process the information swirling around the body—the different textures, the concrete and the sky, the bricks and the trees, the dwindling procession of sounds, the damping of decibels, the botanical sigh of the grass swaying in the wind, the comings and goings of the traffic around her, speeding up and slowing down. It strikes her how calm the hotel employees are; one of them lights a cigarette, inhales, then blows out a cloud of nicotine, blue curls of smoke hanging briefly in the air.

Out of the corner of her eye, she notices an old woman on the median in the middle of the boulevard crossing herself as a paramedic bends over to drape a thermal blanket over the chest, shoulders and exposed, delicate neck of the woman in Valencia, leaving only her face uncovered. She fixates on the sweat beading on the nape of the man's neck, running down his back and soaking the collar of his pale shirt. Claire doesn't dare ask him if the woman is dead. She imagines she must be, since no one is trying to revive her. There's no blood—or very little, at least—no red pool forming under her skull, but maybe that's because her hair is soaking it up. Claire has seen more blood on her son's sheets when he wakes up with a nosebleed in the middle of the night. She examines the stranger's legs, focusing on the thighs, knees and calves sticking out from under the reflective blanket, unable to linger on the mutilated foot for more than a second. She'll never forget the woman's skin. It looks so smooth, so flat, inanimate. The exquisiteness of flawless skin, or maybe it's just rigor. It's hard to tell if she's wearing ultra-sheer pantyhose or if her skin really is that lustrous and perfect. There's no redness, no glow, no tan lines. Just a horrifyingly even texture, bizarre and deathlike, unreal. It's more like faux flesh, the kind you'd see on the mannequins displayed in a shop window or the wax dolls that old ladies keep locked away behind glass.

———

Claire doesn't wait for them to take the body away; she goes back upstairs to join her husband and children at the pool. Their daughter is demanding to be taken to the park, which they'd promised her earlier that day.

She's jumping up and down impatiently, waving her arms and legs in the air: A picnic, I want a picnic! Claire swallows slowly, then meets Jean's worried gaze with a level stare. In a flat, even voice, she says: Okay, let's have a picnic, let's go up to the room and fix the sandwiches and veggies. In their hotel room, she throws up bile in the toilet while Jean tries to distract the children.

They set out together for Benicalap Park. They walk around the left side of the hotel, toward the back of the building, to avoid the spot where the woman hit the ground. They take the long way to the park, hoping the motion of the stroller will coax their son to sleep for his afternoon nap. They don't speak. The silence is broken only by the squeaking of the stroller wheels turning on their rusty axis. The area is mostly deserted, with nothing but indistinct plots of land, a vacant lot, a rundown building covered with graffiti. It's grey, dirty, overgrown. There are a few traces of human life lying around: scraps of fabric, empty beer cans, cigarette butts, a discarded chair. Claire wonders if the woman came from this hostile no man's land. It's no place for tourists or a family stroll, with a six-year-old girl trailing by the hand and a toddler nodding off against the bright orange canvas of his stroller, which, along with his sister's fuchsia dress, is the only splash of colour anywhere around.

When Claire thinks back to that picnic, the taste of raw carrots is the main thing she remembers. A mouthful of dry, stringy bits sliding around under her tongue, knocking against her molars, breaking up under her canines, and finally rolling toward her uvula. The pieces of carrot stick in her throat, scratch the roof of her mouth, cut off her air supply.

Months, even years later, miles away from Benicalap Park, whenever she bites into a carrot, Claire Halde will still be thinking about the woman in Valencia as she chews. It hurts to swallow; even after all that time, she comes perilously close to choking.

———

Back from the picnic, after bathing the kids and putting them to bed, Claire goes to the hotel gym, just off the pool. She's not brave enough this time to go for a run in the city.

Claire Halde puts one foot in front of the other, closing in on eight kilometres running in place in front of the mirror in the deserted gym. This is her first time running on a treadmill. She's wobbly at first, thrown off kilter trying to adjust her pace to the regular, mechanical motion under her feet, but she eventually hits her stride, finds a certain confidence. *Don't slip, don't trip, don't fall.* On the smooth, unbroken black belt, with just enough cracks and crevices to give it some grip, she eats up the miles. Claire pushes an arrow and the machine beep, beep, beeps like an oven timer; the black belt spins faster, there's a whooshing noise, a loud revving like a plane taking off, her shoes skim the surface and the rubber squeaks. *Run, run, run, keep moving.* She watches her time and pace on the chest-high screen in front of her, between her fists, which she swings back and forth like a boxer, level with her pounding heart, which is pumping blood in quick, steady beats.

There's a message scrolling by in narrow green electronic lettering: *Wellness significa equilibrio mental.* The motor hums like the drone of a sewing machine or the frenzied thwack-thwack of windshield wipers on high speed, and Claire's soles hammer the treadmill sharply while a tubby cleaning lady chases dust bunnies behind her. The gym is closing soon.

She has no clue that I let another woman die, thinks Claire Halde. She forces herself to smile at the housekeeper in the mirror. In the past few hours, smiling has become a chore. The hotel employee turns up the corners of her mouth by way of an acknowledgement. Her eyes are slanted, her movements slow. Maybe she's the one who had to mop up the blood and scrub down the washroom on the fourth floor, Claire thinks, upping her speed another notch.

For a split second, almost like a hallucination, a pair of waxy legs flashes across the mirror, tricking her into thinking someone has just walked into the room. Claire jumps, startled, and the legs disappear. She glances behind her, then clamps her eyes on the mirror like someone surveying the sky after thinking they've just seen a flash of lightning, tensed for the next bolt. She clings to the machine as the cleaning lady watches her surreptitiously, makes eye contact in the mirror, then lowers her gaze back to her rag. Her face is round, shuttered, focused on her work, which she does with indifference, as employees often do when forced to carry out repetitive tasks.

She approaches with her aerosol can, shaking it vigorously. The metal cylinder rattles like it's filled with nails. Claire flashes back to her childhood, in a time before the hole in the ozone layer: the satisfying machine-gun sound when she would help her mother clean the windows, her father's chin covered in shaving cream, her and her sister fighting over who would get to spray the fake Christmas tree with canned snow. Rat-a-tat-tat, followed by a long hissing sound and a cloud of particles released into the room, floating through the air, sticking in Claire's throat. The foam cleaner, thick and white, expands and froths on contact with the mirror. The breathless runner's reflection quickly disappears behind a snowy cloud of chemical foam.

Claire Halde goes back to her room, where she steps under the powerful jets of the rainfall showerhead, directly under the large disk dotted with tiny pinholes. She looks down at the rectangular bar of soap nestled in her palm. On contact with the water, fragrant, olive-green suds form on its surface. She's relying on this late-night shower to calm her down and ease her into sleep. She relaxes slightly, rolls her shoulders, squeezes her shoulder blades together and releases the tension in her neck under the scalding water. The urge to cry hits her as violently as the need to sneeze; she thinks she might pass out in the suffocating steam, but she doesn't care. The water plasters her hair to her forehead in hot, ropy clumps, but she doesn't push them away. She has trouble opening her eyes against the force of the jets. The water runs into her mouth, gets up her nose, pools at her feet. In a sudden fit, Claire attacks her body with the miniature bar of soap, leaving her skin red in places. The sharp ridges of the soap rub painfully against her less fleshy bits: armpits, neck, backs of knees, anklebones, shins and wrists.

THE HOTEL AT NIGHT

It's nighttime now. The day began with the intricate ballet of the phosphorescent jellyfish, the pirouettes of the dolphins, the amazement of the children—mouths agape, little hands pressed up against the glass of the tanks, dwarfed by the giant sea creatures, screeching with joy whenever a school of fish glided by—and it's ended with the death of a woman replaying in a loop, sleep that won't come, guilt, waves of nausea.

The images of the blonde woman twitching on the sidewalk have snuffed out all the magic of the Oceanogràfic. Her breath coming in gasps, Claire dissects the afternoon's events minute by minute, from the stranger's arrival at the pool to the chunk of heel bone lying on the pavement. Claire sees the woman walking toward her in slow motion, like a psychedelic catwalk performance or an actress in a *film noir*—Lynchian, Hitchcockesque. Her skeletal frame, her posture, shaky and distraught, a flash, then the sequence on fast forward: blonde hair, hoarse voice, waxy legs, white cotton square, oversized purse, hand struggling with zipper, cigarette trembling between lips, blood soaking through dressing, dripping down wrist onto blue towel, body slipping over edge of roof, scream trapped in throat, lungs devoid of air, elevator ride, spasms on sidewalk, chunk of bone and apricot-coloured flesh, ambulance siren, emergency blanket, sign of cross on median, taste of dirt in mouth, little girl hopping up and down, vomit, raw carrots.

In the hotel room, three sleeping bodies and her own rigid, restless one. Three bodies that have been inside her own: the two babies she carried in her belly, grown into small children slumbering in the wide hotel bed, little cheeks pressed up against an oversized feather pillow, the stiff, white cotton warmed by their moist breath; and the man who has caressed her, licked her, bitten her, penetrated her, made her scream and come, her neck, shoulders and pelvis spasming with brief and intense waves of pleasure. These three bodies have drifted off to sleep, while in Claire's head, dark and terrifying fish slither through her thoughts. She sits motionless in the armchair next to the window, knees bent, heels pressed into her bottom, fingers laced around her shins, in a pitiful fetal position. Stomach still heaving, on the verge of vomiting at any second—a flashback to her first trimester with both kids—she digs her nails into the delicate skin of her palms, into the crevice between life line and head line.

She watches the children sleep, moved by the peaceful sound of their baby snores, comforted by the reassuring symphony of untroubled sleep. She'd know that breathing anywhere, that downy rising and falling that had soothed her when her babies had fallen asleep at her breast or dozed off in her arms for their afternoon nap, the tiny sounds of slumber and repose that have changed little over the years. Jean's sleep, with its distinctive patterns, restlessness, and grunts and groans, is different. Unlike a milk-drunk infant, when he's had too much to drink, his breathing gets loud and annoying. Claire elbows him in the side, but it's about as effective as trying to shift an animal that's been shot with a tranquilizer dart. The unyielding body next to her feels completely foreign.

Memories of nights spent nursing float to the surface. This is the same silence, enveloped in a deeper silence, the same kind of sleep that surrounds her now. She can picture herself walking into the kitchen in the middle of the night, parking herself in front of the fridge and opening the door with an exhausted jerk. After the predictable click of the rubber gasket unsticking and the lightbulb switching on above the top shelf, she'd stand immobile in the square of light, contemplating the contents, lulled by the drone of the motor. In this room, now, she feels like she did standing in the glow of that open door when, half-naked and famished, she'd eat yogurt straight from the container, hoping against hope that the newborn she'd just put down in the bassinette would sleep through the rest of the night without demanding another feeding. Those dimly lit hours of maternal solitude were much like the ones ticking by now in this hotel room; the night eddied with the same currents of worry and fatigue, and the feeling of not being a good enough mother, woman, lover, daughter. That numbness that pervades your whole body and clouds your vision, when your skin feels like it's weighed down by a layer of clay, when staring into the soft glow of a lightbulb sends you into a trance, and you're suddenly convinced of the need to take stock of your entire life, right there, in the middle of the night.

ROOM 714

In the silent room, in the hollow Valencian night, far removed from everything, as though the Valencia Palace has come unmoored and is now adrift on dark waters, Claire still can't sleep.

In her insomnia, she recalls the pair of vacationers lounging on their deck chairs at the far end of the terrace. They never even noticed the woman in Valencia, never saw her bleeding or her body falling from the roof. They had no clue what was going on, Claire thinks, never heard her weak cry of horror. They'll return home well rested, oblivious to what happened, happy with their trip to Spain. *But why did she choose me? Those two could have probably helped her.* And that's when Claire finally starts to cry.

What follows are several nights of sharks and screams, the woman's voice, the edge of a roof, her daughter's hand slipping from her grasp, falls into the void, and sweaty jolts awake, with the woman's dull, lifeless stare imprinted on her retina.

⁓

Claire lifts the stiff, heavy duvet and slides one leg out without disturbing the mattress. She's an expert at getting out of bed without waking Jean. They've been on different sleep cycles for years now. They may share the same snug cotton cocoon, but they each have their own way of responding to the heat—Jean by sweating and Claire by waking up constantly. Nestled in this unfamiliar bed, where others have lain before them, enjoying the comfortable pocket-coil mattress and cursing the itchy feathers poking out of the hotel-issue duvet, they lie apart, not touching, curled up on separate sides of the bed. The years when they used to make passionate love, veering off hiking trails in pursuit of simultaneous orgasms in fields or on clifftops overlooking the river, waking up at night to start all over again, are nothing but a distant memory. Now, when Claire looks at Jean's naked body, she feels resignation rather than desire. She makes love to him the same way she sorts the recycling and puts out and rinses the bin every Monday morning: out of obligation, like a household chore that needs doing.

The mattress doesn't make a sound as Claire places one foot on the carpet. The alarm clock reads 3:04 a.m. She slips her feet into her sandals, pulls a sheet up over a child's arm and drapes her navy cardigan over her shoulders, buttoning it up crookedly over her nightgown. As she walks toward the door, she presses a hand to her side; through the ribbing of the sweater, she can feel the rectangular shape of the woman in Valencia's key card, which she'd stashed in the pocket. She retraces her steps, gropes around on the dresser for her own key, emblazoned with the hotel logo, and folds it, smooth and cold, into her palm. Ever so gently, like she's caressing a child's cheek, she turns the lever until she hears the muted click of the latch releasing. Claire closes the door slowly behind her and steps out into the hallway.

She makes her way down the stairs to the fourth floor. She's careful to close the heavy fire door behind her, then pauses for a moment in the hallway, which looks exactly like every other hallway in the Valencia Palace Hotel, with its mocha carpeting and cream-coloured panelling interspersed with expanses of vaguely walnut-looking faux wood around each door. Spotlights on the ceiling and knee-high emergency lighting strips cast an intense, hazy glow, almost like they were designed to hurry guests back to their rooms. But Claire lingers; she approaches a door, presses her ear up against it, holds her breath. She runs a hand slowly over the smooth, shiny surface of the artificial wood, traces a finger around the fake knots and imitation rings, lined up in a predictable horizontal pattern, there to give the impression of the real thing, but not fooling anyone.

The walls are perfectly soundproofed. It's impossible to tell which rooms are occupied, who's sleeping, who's having sex, who's battling insomnia or infidelity or depression, who's masturbating, who can't get it up, who's snoring, who feels utterly alone behind these impenetrable doors, locked tight with an electronic bolt. A rabbit hutch made up of perfectly aligned cages, with thick concrete walls designed to block out all sound, ensure a peaceful night's sleep. She tiptoes forward, coming to a stop in front of one of the rooms, hyperaware of the silence, the night, the muted tones of the hallway. She spends a few seconds turning the woman in Valencia's key card over and over in her fingers, as though preparing for a coin toss. She slides it into the slot in the waist-high door handle and swipes down. The light stays red. Claire pivots and tries the lock on the door across the hall. Nothing happens. She keeps going, making her way along the nubby wall-to-wall carpeting, card in hand, heart in her throat each time she slides the key into the narrow slot on one of the doors. Her palm is sweating, her temples pounding. The risk is intoxicating, like slipping into a cage with a predator or reaching out to stroke a big cat.

Another step, another door.

At the second-to-last door on the left, against all expectations, the light turns green and a click breaks the silence. Claire freezes, a lump of fear in her throat. She hesitates between running away and slowly pushing the door open; for a second, she remains mired between the two, on the razor's edge.

Then, powerless to resist, Claire eases the door open on its hinges. She takes one step forward, and the floor suddenly gives way. She loses her footing and she's about to go over a cliff, into a bottomless pit, the start of a sickening fall through the Valencian sky, through the oppressive night air. She topples into the void, her body in free fall. She sees her reflection streaking by in the windows of the Valencia Palace Hotel; she's blonde and terrified, she doesn't recognize herself. With mere inches to go before she hits the ground, she screams and sits bolt upright in bed, her back drenched with sweat in the frigid hotel room. Jean moans quietly, rolls over and wraps himself in the sheet, while Claire stares wide-eyed at the white soundproof ceiling, tries to steady her breathing and go back to sleep.

———

Someone other than her, Claire Halde tortures herself, might have been more helpful, might have reacted better or been more comforting in the time it would have taken to call for help or come to the strange woman's assistance. Surely, someone else would have said or done the right thing at the right time, offered her a warm smile, an "it'll be okay" or a "don't worry, we'll take care of you," a glimmer of hope, a measure of kindness in the form of a smile or a hand on the small of her back, with the compassion needed or the wherewithal required to shield the woman from her own desperation, from her determination to depart this world.

Claire Halde will keep this story from her friends and family, and Jean will eventually tell her that he's sick of hearing about it. She will carry the secret around like a vicious scar, and the encounter in Valencia will become engraved on her mind. A crack in the heretofore smooth finish, a defect, a burden, a sense of self-loathing, the biggest failure of her life. In the wake of the woman's death, she will hand herself down a sentence of silence and self-effacement and something resembling guilt.

And yet, she didn't kill the woman. No one will come to arrest her or even question her. She didn't run over a child with her car. She didn't lose control of her vehicle, spin out on the highway, commit a hit-and-run or mow down strangers in a moment of distraction. She didn't start a forest fire, burn down a parliament building, torture an animal, smuggle ivory in her suitcase or plan a terrorist attack.

Up to that point, Claire Halde had lived a life virtually above reproach. She carried her elderly neighbour's shopping bags into the house and shovelled her driveway during the winter, she often held out her arm to a young blind man on his way to the metro, she always stopped at crosswalks, always used her flashers, rarely gave in to road rage. She even let the squeegee kids make a streaky mess of her windshield in exchange for a few coins, which she handed over with a smile. She often asked the homeless man bundled up in front of the grocery store if she could buy him a meal, beaming with pride at the sight of her generous, kind-hearted children holding out a barbecued chicken, a carton of milk or chocolate cookies to the man with the sunken, hollow cheeks—*Mama, can we give him a little treat today?* She also gave money to the rubby who held the door open for her at the Fabre metro station and to the gypsy woman in front of the Asian market with the passel of snot-nosed kids clinging to her embroidered skirts, although less often, mostly because she couldn't stand it when people used their kids to attract sympathy. For the same reason, she never gave a cent to some charities, but gave generously to others, like Doctors Without Borders and Amnesty International. She even gave up her seat in the metro for old people and pregnant ladies. But, for that desperate woman in Valencia, she'd had nothing but cold indifference.

DAY 3 ITINERARY

At breakfast, the children are impressed by the buffet in the hotel restaurant. They pile their plates high with pastries, ham, eggs and jam. Jean eats with gusto, sipping his coffee while paging through a guidebook. He plans the day ahead. The children go back for seconds. Claire forces herself to swallow a few bites, chews slowly, with no real interest in her food. She drinks two big cups of coffee while watching the people eating at the surrounding tables. The hotel staff are cheerful. The guests are relaxed. You'd never know a woman killed herself at this very hotel the night before. The newspapers don't even mention her death.

Checkout is at noon. After breakfast, the kids ask to go for a swim; they want to enjoy the pool for as long as possible. Jean agrees to take them and suggests that Claire go for a run to clear her head.

When she hits the streets of Valencia that morning, Claire Halde feels detached from reality, like she's running outside her own body. The streets, the buildings, the pedestrians she deftly avoids—seniors, the odd couple with arms wrapped around each other's waists, babies in strollers, roly-poly little girls like her daughter playing hopscotch—it all flashes by in a haze. Nothing but vague shapes stand out from among the Valencian cityscape; she runs with just enough focus to avoid obstacles and cracks, to stop obediently for red lights, to watch out for reckless drivers. It's the same easy motion as when she runs at home, in her own city, on the streets and paths so familiar to her. Her body moves forward on autopilot in Valencia, speeding up and switching gears smoothly, but her thoughts are detached and her concentration almost nonexistent. And yet, she runs to feel alive; she pounds the pavement to numb the part of her brain where her conscience and her obsessions dwell.

WORTH THE DETOUR:
THE VALENCIA INSTITUTE OF MODERN ART

They check out at noon, right on time, after showering quickly and shoving wet bathing suits and sweaty workout gear in a plastic bag, which they tuck into the suitcase at the last minute. They stow their luggage in a locker at the train station, then walk over to the Valencia Institute of Modern Art, where they will spend the afternoon before taking the train back to Barcelona.

They begin their tour with the *Lived Body* exhibit, and the children twitter nervously in front of the photos that show genitals, breasts and shrivelled skin, which they're not used to seeing. Claire sits on a navy blue bench in a dark room; jaw clenched, she watches a series of slides projected on the white wall. Nan Goldin's *The Ballad of Sexual Dependency* leaves her breathless. She experiences the images like a punch in the gut: the bodies of the men, women and children, bones protruding, skin smooth and bright on some, battered and bruised on others, their injuries and their smiles, their embraces, their eyes suffused with desire or hopelessness or contentment. She is struck by how the light imbues them with a sense of poignancy, fallibility, humanity.

Watching the slides and listening to the music that accompanies the portraits provides her with a measure of comfort, a feeling of consolation that eases the sorrow she's felt since the day before.

Jean leaves the room well before the end, continuing on his way with the kids, but Claire stays for the rest of *The Ballad*, not wanting to miss anything, transfixed by the slideshow as though it were a family album conjuring up long-forgotten memories.

PUERTA DE SERRANOS

After the museum, they still have time for one more attraction before they're due to catch their train. Jean climbs to the top of Puerta de Serranos with their daughter, while Claire stays down below with the little guy, who's fast asleep. She doesn't have the stomach for heights right now, and it's all she can do to keep it together for the kids, going through the motions of motherhood: tying a shoelace, buttoning a shirt, washing hands, combing hair, pushing the stroller, holding her daughter's hand as they cross the street.

The little girl waves at her from the top of one of the massive Gothic towers, happy and carefree. Her father has picked her up by the waist, and she's leaning over the stone rampart, in one of the crenellations, to get a better look at her mother and brother far below. Claire's legs give out from under her and she crumples to the ground, head between her knees, clutching the stroller wheel for balance.

From that moment on, everywhere Claire Halde looks, she will see bodies raining down from the sky.

THE TRAIN RIDE

Claire makes her way slowly down the aisle. There are a few passengers scattered around the carriage, people dozing off, an elderly couple. The mauve purse knocks against her hip, and she clutches it protectively against her body. She turns around, tries to catch Jean's eye. He's slipped an arm around their little boy, who's dozing on his chest. On the seat across from them, their daughter has also fallen asleep, her head resting against the window on a makeshift sweater-pillow.

The bathrooms are tucked between two cars. Claire pushes open the accordion door, slides the lock into place and hangs the bag on the wall hook. The sound emanating from the train to Barcelona is monotonous, steady, predictable. There's an announcement: *We'll be arriving at the station in twenty-five minutes.* Claire runs the water for a minute, lets it fill her cupped palms, splashes it on her face. She tucks a stray strand of hair back into her bun, unbuttons her sweater, straightens her blouse.

She opens the purse and grabs a frosted makeup case. She takes out a tube of lipstick and removes the gold lid. In the rectangular mirror, Claire surveys herself closely as she paints her lips with several coats of the woman in Valencia's lipstick, a creamy blood red that's started to melt in the heat. Claire stares at her reflection, puckering and smacking her lips together. You can't miss them—her shiny, luscious lips, bright as a maraschino cherry. She lines the sink delicately with a paper towel, as though preparing to lay out syringes, a round mirror and other dental instruments. She arranges the various cosmetics with care: blush, eyeshadow, eyeliner, mascara and face powder, which she applies in succession to the apples of her cheeks, the creases of her eyelids, the full length of her lashes, the stubborn oily spot on her forehead. She smiles at herself mechanically in the mirror, sizes herself up as she would a stranger who both fascinates and repulses her. The jerky movements of the train throw her off balance just as she's having another go with the eyeliner. A thick, black line shoots across her eyelid, like a jagged seam reducing her eye to a slit. Doe-eye fail. She rips off a length of toilet paper, which she raises to her mouth to wipe away the red, rubbing so hard she tears the thin, delicate tissue of her lips, drawing blood. The skin around her mouth turns pink, like a wound healing over.

She puts away the makeup and closes the case, then bundles it in the folds of her cardigan. She eyes the purse as it swings back and forth on the hook, vibrating with the motion of the train.

BACK IN BARCELONA

In the days following their return to Barcelona, her blood turns to ice whenever she hears the wail of an ambulance siren.

Claire is terrified that she'll never get over it, that she'll slide irretrievably into obscurity, the unknown, her own indifference.

She chokes down her fears and her guilty thoughts, does her best to make up for her many silences by plastering a weak smile on her face. She suppresses her sighs and puts on her vacation face, mostly for the kids.

SITGES

The Sunday after the fall, a few days before returning to Montreal, as they're strolling along the shore in Sitges—"Must-see seaside resort," according to the guidebooks—Claire notices a woman sit down on a stone palisade overlooking a cliff. As Claire looks on, the woman shifts her weight onto her hands and raises her legs. Claire stops dead in the middle of the street, drops her little girl's hand, shakes her head. Her entire body freezes. She takes a step forward, ready to sprint toward the cliff, and just as she frantically screams STOP!, she realizes the woman is smiling. Her head is at a forty-five degree angle, and she's pushed her sunglasses onto the top of her head, which is covered with a thick helmet of dull, brown hair. The woman is posing for her husband, a sweaty, oily-faced man in Bermuda shorts, holding a camera not six feet away. Claire trembles as she takes her daughter's hand again, and Jean glares at her, eyebrows furrowed.

"What the hell, Claire?"

"I don't know, I just thought..."

MONTREAL AIRPORT

At carousel 6, they're still waiting for their luggage to emerge. People are getting impatient. Some look visibly annoyed, foreheads creased with frown lines; others are huffing and puffing, taking their exasperation out on their life or travel partner: Talk about a crappy ending to our holiday, what a shitty company, worst experience of my life, we should make a complaint. Jean crosses his arms and exhales loudly; he casts an irritated glance at the kids, who are standing next to the conveyor belt, waiting eagerly for the suitcases to appear. Claire keeps her distance, hangs back from the crowd; quite frankly, she'd like to walk away from the whole scene. She looks away. Her gaze travels above the roiling sea of peeved heads and shoulders and comes to rest on a giant TV tuned to a twenty-four-hour news channel. Headlines scroll by on a blue ticker at the bottom of the screen: "New surge of violence in Sudan. Young woman found in California 18 years after kidnapping. Teenage girl drowns in Rimouski River. Montreal beats record high set 83 years ago."

Later, as Claire is looking out the window at the cars crawling by on the Metropolitan, another news bulletin will announce the latest in a string of tragedies in the Mediterranean. Libyan authorities have found the bodies of one hundred and thirteen migrants washed up on shore after their boat capsized off the coast of Sicily, the radio announcer will drone. It's estimated that some one hundred others may have gone down with the ship, she'll conclude, before moving on to the sports scores, the weather, the arts and entertainment segment, and finally the traffic. At that point, the taxi driver will turn up the volume and let out a long, weary sigh. Claire and

Jean will look at each other silently in the air-conditioned car. Drivers will need to be patient: It's going to be another long ride home.

―

Over the years, various news stories she reads will continue to raise the spectre of the woman in Valencia. "Man throws himself off Tate Modern," a headline will blare one July afternoon. A woman will confess to the *Evening Standard* that she finds it "really sad that this happened on the first sunny day of the year and just before the Olympics." Memories of the Spanish city will come surging back with news of an investigation into how a drunk man died after being struck in the head by a metro train at the Langelier station one January evening. Sprawled out on the platform, he was ignored by at least forty bystanders and three transit employees. No one lifted a finger to help him as two metros came and went, mere inches from his body, as a full sixteen minutes elapsed, and the man lay dying without anyone raising an eyebrow. When Winston Moseley, Kitty Genovese's killer, dies in prison at the age of eighty-one, more than half a century after brutally raping and murdering her in the middle of a New York City street, Claire Halde will read old newspaper articles about how thirty-eight witnesses watched the scene unfold from their apartment windows without coming to the victim's rescue.

At night, too, she will be haunted by the outline of the woman's body—that skin and that blonde hair. The unrelentingly hoarse and garbled voice will penetrate her nightmares. And when she's running—months, even years after the trip to Valencia—she'll sometimes feel a dull throbbing, a jarring sensation in her heel bone. Never again will she be able to hear the word *Valencia* without thinking about the woman, without reminding herself: While on vacation in Spain, you let someone die.

II

RETURN TO VALENCIA
(The hostile point on the horizon)

THINGS TO DO BEFORE YOU DIE

I remember my mother running.

I think about her often, sprinting like she was trying to escape from us, run away from us at top speed.

Since arriving in Spain three days ago, I've been carrying around the same soft-cover notebook with the mustard-yellow binding. I run my hand over its smooth surface; I'm too scared to read it again. I'm keeping my distance.

Over the years, my mother amassed countless of these slim notebooks, which she bought from a Japanese stationery store in New York City. When I turned eighteen, my father gave me a pile of them, most of them identical, all of them dog-eared to varying degrees. There's a rectangular sticker on the cover of one of them, the same kind she used to label our school workbooks and Duo-Tangs. In the blank space framed by a thin blue border, she'd written in cursive, in black ink: "Trip to Spain." Tucked between the pages, on a sheet of paper folded in four, I found a list of bullet points, all starting with an asterisk and lined up neatly under the heading "Things To Do Before I Die."

I've read that list from the late 2000s several times in the past few months. I was still in elementary school back then. It's weird to think about her adding an item that involved me: "Run a marathon with one of my kids (maybe as my fiftieth-birthday present from them?)."

In my first apartment, near Little Italy, where I grew up, I hung a large, glossy 11 x 17 photo. In it, I'm six years old and there's a *P'tit marathon de Montréal* bib pinned to my dark grey hoodie. Two long braids are splayed out in midair around my face, which is screwed up in effort. My eyes are fixed on the finish line, my forehead determined, my fists clenched. My mother, who's running next to me, isn't touching the ground; she's suspended in a ray of light, her Adidas hovering over the asphalt and a carpet of dead leaves. She's smiling at me proudly, as though she considered running a state of grace. *There's something unreal about your mom in this picture.* Everyone who dropped by my place was struck by my rosy-cheeked, floating mom in motion—from her dazzling smile and ferocious look to her muscular calves emerging from form-fitting, electric-blue capri pants—every inch of her screaming: Run, sweetheart, you can do it!

I keep her many finisher medals from the Paris, London, Tokyo, New York City, Berlin, San Francisco and Boston marathons in one of my dresser drawers, hidden under a jumble of underwear. Whenever I'm rummaging around, half-naked, for a pair of nylons or flimsy lace panties, my fingers get caught up in the satin ribbons and the medals all jangle together. The clinking and clanging might as well be the sound of all the years that have passed, marked by a jeering brass band. I run my hand along the bottom of the drawer, finger the metal one more time, just to make sure the mementoes are still there—cold, sonorous disks buried under piles of white cotton and satin bras. I press them against my palm: the miniature skyscrapers of Manhattan and Tokyo, the Brandenburg Gate, Big Ben, the Golden Gate Bridge. When the medals rub up against one another, the embossed designs emit a shrill sound, like the singing of a cicada, filling my room with a preternatural cry, insistent and hypnotic.

My mother, fifty this month.

We didn't set off fireworks over the lake like we did for her fortieth. But, in a few minutes, a starter's pistol will be fired into the milky sky, and that burst will signal the start of the 2025 Valencia Marathon.

I will run this marathon—my first—as though my mother were next to me the whole time.

THE WEATHER OUTSIDE

It's a rainy Sunday, ten years earlier. It's exactly noon, Eastern Standard Time, according to the radio, which has been broadcasting the National Research Council of Canada's official radio time signal every day since the Second World War. The summer storm lashing Montreal is more violent than the meteorologists had predicted. Strong enough to uproot trees and cause the river to burst its banks. In the Laurentians, power lines are toppling like dominoes. Bits of roofing shingles are hurtling through the sky, which is devoid of planes, because they've all been grounded. Even more than the disgruntled travellers staring up at the departure boards, Montreal drivers are edgy and impatient. Cursing, they've been jammed up in detours for hours because a cycling event—which will be called off abruptly due to the high winds—has shut down traffic across much of the city.

Seated in a tearoom, her back to the window and oblivious to all this, Claire slowly swallows her last sip of a cup of Earl Grey that's gone cold. She's sitting across from a girlfriend who's got a better vantage of the sky.

"It's completely black out there now. We'd better get home quick."

"Yeah. Anyways, they're waiting on me for supper."

Claire calls home: Put the water on, I'm on my way. She runs home at a clip, the tepid, murky water splashing up the backs of her thighs.

She stops at a red light, sees her standing at the gas station.

She's wearing a skintight miniskirt and a tank top that's sliding down one shoulder, revealing the top half of a braless, saggy breast. She's gesticulating in the middle of the street, purse swinging from her wrist, paying no mind to the traffic. Drivers honk at her and brake abruptly, throwing a curtain of muddy water over her trembling figure. Cars swerve around her, then drive off again into the storm. Her hair is thick and black, like steel wool. Her arms are scrawny and restless, whipping back and forth wildly through the air and water, like the antennae of a frenzied insect. The rain streams over her eyelids, which are blinking open and closed like someone in the throes of an epileptic seizure. She's obviously high. The jerky movements of her arms and legs and the spasms contorting her face trigger a sudden flashback of the woman on the rooftop terrace.

Valencia. The feelings of impotence and imminent danger, buried deep inside her body for almost six years

83

now, come rushing to the fore. Claire surveys her surroundings. There's no one around. The rain-drenched sidewalks are deserted, no Good Samaritan steps out of his car or rushes out of the coffee shop across the street. The gas station attendant remains behind his bulletproof window, keeping an eye on his till. Claire and the woman are completely alone. Like a freak tidal wave, the memory of the Valencia Palace rises up and threatens to overcome her. For a moment, the horizon disappears behind a black wall of water.

It's not unheard of for an aftershock to be stronger than the original earthquake. Memories rise up with a force that threatens to drown her: a delayed reaction to a shock already several years old. She feels like she's just been shot up with a thick, sticky liquid that's turning her veins to ice and stopping up the walls of her throat, stomach and skull.

Claire takes a few steps forward in the street, up to her ankles in water, lungs filled with lead. Her body is rocked by a powerful wave, like her brain is a gas pump and the automatic shutoff valve has just malfunctioned. She's caught off guard, doesn't see it coming. Maybe it's toxic fumes slithering down her airways or fuel gushing up from the huge underground tanks under her feet, cracking the pavement and creeping up her legs, coating her from head to toe. *I'm a seagull trapped in a slick, black tide, in the wrong place at the wrong time again.* She wants to scream: Watch out! But great bubbles of oil and tar, and a pocket of air under her tongue, prevent the words from escaping, transforming the scream into some otherworldly sound.

The woman turns to look at her and squints as though trying to place her. She walks toward Claire. The stilted gait, the uneven swaying of the hips, the wobbly head, the immeasurable solitude in the face of danger: It's all identical. Claire is reliving the events of Valencia at top speed. But she shakes it off. This time, she'll say something. Do something.

She motions to the woman to step back onto the sidewalk.

"What do you want from me?" the woman screams as she approaches.

"Come here, get on the sidewalk. No, not the street. Stay here with me."

The woman gives her a withering look, but Claire insists.

"Please come here. You'll be killed if you don't get off the street."

Muttering nonsense, the stranger pitches forward and reaches out an arm to Claire, who takes a step back, afraid the woman might hit or punch her. Claire doesn't trust her; she's acting unpredictably, ranting and waving her fist in the air, not to mention that she's two heads taller than Claire is. But the woman veers away and sits down on a cement block.

Fingers trembling, Claire struggles to dial 911 on the wet screen of her mobile while never once taking her eyes off the woman, who gets up and staggers toward the busy street through the sheeting rain.

The 911 dispatcher assesses the emergency, notes down the intersection. The woman throws herself in front of a car—Oh, my god! Get back here!—which just barely avoids her. Claire gestures at her wildly and tries her best to attract her attention while the dispatcher repeats his question impatiently:

"Ma'am, ma'am, answer me: What is she wearing?"

"Sorry," Claire begins flatly, "it's just that I'm trying to—"

"Ma'am," he cuts her off, "just answer the question. Describe her clothes for me."

"Black skirt and tank top, tall, dark hair. And she's carrying a purse... Do I think she's dangerous?" she continues, still watching the woman, who's now rubbing her face vigorously. "Well, she might cause an accident or be hit by a car. I think she's high."

"Someone else has already called this in. The police are on their way," the dispatcher concludes, no less brusquely.

Soon after, a young man runs up to Claire and explains that he went to get a patrol car stationed a block away for the cycling event. With the confidence of someone swooping in to save the day, which frankly blows Claire's mind, he walks up to the woman:

"Come sit down by the gas station, get out of the rain, the taxi's on its way."

He's soon joined by two friends, and they surround the woman, who sits down on a concrete curb under the gas pump awning. Claire explains that she has to go and runs off into the rain, which is picking up again in intensity, like the burning feeling in her stomach.

When she arrives home, soaked to the bone, looking like a drowned rat, she notices that the kids have set the table, dished out the spaghetti, grated the parmesan, filled a pitcher with water. Claire isn't hungry; she crawls into bed without even taking off her wet clothes and lies there trembling uncontrollably.

I'm a mess, she thinks, for the first time in her life. The shakes and wracking sobs last for two hours; in the midst of it all, she's horrified to realize she hasn't cried like this in years, not since room 714 in Valencia.

"Lucky Strikes," she says a few hours later to the cashier at the gas station, after getting the kids to bed and slipping out. "You don't have any? I don't know then, the cheapest pack you've got. King size, with a lighter."

She slides a twenty into the slot between the window and the counter. "So, did they finally call an ambulance for that woman this afternoon?" she asks, jutting her chin in the direction of the street out front. The man nods and hands her the cigarettes. Claire, who's never been a smoker, caresses the pack, runs a finger gently over the lighter, which is bright pink like the colour of corned beef.

"It was you, on the sidewalk with her? I saw you. Good thing you were there. One less dead person today thanks to you."

Claire grabs her change and walks out without so much as a goodbye.

2025 VALENCIA MARATHON:
STARTING LINE

All around me, the runners are jumping in place, double-knotting their shoelaces, sighing nervously, smiling at one another. According to the organizers, there are twenty-four thousand participants gathered at the starting line. They're all just standing there, waiting; some are stamping their feet. They're like a school of frenzied sardines, excited and anxious in their flashy, synthetic running gear. The *Valencia Ciudad del Running* banners flap in the wind. Off to one side, there's the Palau de les Arts Reina Sofía, an ultramodern opera house that looks like it's floating over the reflecting pools below. I think about my father, about see-through glass bridges. Santiago Calatrava is one of his favourite architects. On my right, the Hemisfèric stares down at the marathoners like an enormous white eye. Some tilt their heads from side to side to stretch their neck muscles; others shake their arms out by their sides, stirring imaginary water with their fingertips. Like a bunch of octopuses. I stand still, nervous but motionless, dormant at the bottom of a frozen lake.

I conserve my energy; I focus on the impending start, on my belly breathing, on the plan: don't start too fast, stay on pace, drink every three kilometres, take an energy gel every forty-five minutes, finish the race with a smile and, above all, think about my mother with each passing kilometre. I close my eyes, take a deep breath. The Valencian air flows down my throat; my ribs lift, my belly expands, then I slowly release the warm air through my nostrils.

I'm all keyed up. I'm thirsty, even though I just drank, and I need to pee. I just want to get started already.

I'm in the middle of the pack, two hundred metres behind the leaders, in corral 9, with the runners who expect to finish in four hours. On my left, there's a man wearing a baseball cap with bunny ears. He's holding a sign above his head that says "00:04:00." Runners gather around him and will do their best not to lose sight of him for the whole 42.2 kilometres.

Four hours—the barrier many amateur runners aim to break. It was also my mother's goal for her first marathon. She didn't make it. She finished the race in four hours three minutes, after fading in the last two kilometres and almost passing out from dehydration at the finish line. My brother and I went to find her with a bottle of water and chocolate milk. We'd imagined her standing triumphantly near the podium. Instead, we'd found her sprawled out on the concrete floor of the stadium, arms flung wide open, her face a sickly shade of green and her mouth ringed with vomit. Her legs were jerking with the force of an epileptic seizure. She'd grabbed on to us so tightly. A desperate embrace, fuelled, I imagine, by the fear of dying, by the terrifying feeling of her body giving out on her. My father had had to pull her to her feet. And yet, after all that, she did it again. Dozens of times more, she faced the marathon head-on, without ever again letting it get the best of her. A few years later, after losing weight and building up her endurance, she was running all her marathons in under three hours thirty minutes. She'd even speed up in the last kilometre, in a final sprint, triumphant in the face of pain. She'd clocked her best time in Berlin, in 2013: three hours eight minutes. Four minutes twenty-seven seconds per kilometre over 42.2 kilometres. I worked it out. I don't know how she managed to be that fast. I can't even keep up that pace over five kilometres.

The announcer's voice booms out excitedly over the loudspeakers, bringing me back to my own marathon.

"*Quinze segons.* Fifteen seconds to go!"

I'm ready. I've trained for sixteen weeks, four times a week: long endurance runs to train my body for fatigue, interval workouts to increase my speed, tempo runs, fartleks, hills, stretching, rest, and carb loading in the days leading up to the marathon. I followed the training program to a tee. My body took it all in, slimmed down, pumped up, adapted. Became accustomed to the constant abuse.

Suddenly, the excitement ratchets up around me.

"*Cinc! Quatre! Tres! Dos! Un!*"

A shot rings out, and the human tide surges forward, trotting at first, docile and impatient.

My heart swells as everyone begins to pick up the pace and move as one toward the starting gate.

KILOMETRE 1

I'm no longer jogging, I'm running, heading toward the Montolivet Bridge, I'm hanging back slightly, on the very edge of the crowd, five minutes fifty seconds per kilometre, the slow start I'd planned, I let the herd shadowing the pace bunny cross the starting line in one tight group, when it's my turn to pass over the electronic mat, I press the button on my stopwatch, and with a tender smile, as though my mother were there with me, I murmur: Happy fiftieth, Mama... C'mon, let's do it, let's run this marathon...

Go, go! You can do it, sweetheart!

... my pulse quickens, it's intoxicating, the excitement at the starting line, I run over the bridge, repeating *don't push it, don't start too fast* over and over, for hundreds of metres, the air pulsates with the sounds of people shouting, rattles shaking, whistles blowing, spectators lean up against the metal barriers, waving signs in the air, and down below, there's *el Río*, the dried-up bed of an erstwhile river, lush gardens, I look straight ahead, breathe calmly, focus inward, I move forward easily, as though the wind were at my back, but it's actually within me, and it's not howling, it's blowing gently, into the farthest reaches of my lungs, it carried my mother along, I know it won't let me down...

KILOMETRE 2

... I'm moving forward, through the roundabout, I spot the "1 KM" marker, the crowd has thinned out, no need to zigzag around the slower runners anymore,

I look down at my watch: five minutes thirty-nine seconds per kilometre, bang on, so far, so good, my legs are strong, my shoulders relaxed, I'm smiling, I'm exactly where I want to be,

making my way through the streets of Valencia, a shiver of excitement like an electric shock sets the hair on the back of my neck on end, stray strands frizz wildly, a thin sheen of sweat forms at the roots, my heart beats steadily, the sky is overcast, ideal,

you used to worry about passing out in the sun, but it makes no difference to me, I like the sun and the shade equally, on my left looms the El Corte Inglés department store, massive and triangular, we're about to turn right onto a street leading to the marina, I've memorized the beginning and the end of the course, the middle is more of a blur...

KILOMETRE 3

... I've been following this woman in the "Cancer Survivor" T-shirt for a while now, I almost feel bad passing her, I smile at her, nod my head in encouragement, she looks so strong and determined, it's hard to imagine her succumbing to a disease, maybe some people are just tougher than others, everyone thought that my mother— who didn't seem afraid of anything, who travelled solo and ran marathons—was stronger than she really was, but we were all wrong, so terribly wrong, you'd never have guessed how fragile she was to look at her, that's what everyone told me, she was an expert at bottling up her emotions and masking her pain, even when she was on the verge of cracking, when she felt like she was being impaled by a cold, hard spear of anxiety through her chest, she ran a marathon full-tilt, finishing first among the women in her age category...

... yet, every time she held a knife to cut carrots for our school lunches, or drove on the highway, or ran over bridges, or stood waiting on the platform for the metro, or stared out the cottage window at the thin ice on the lake, she was thinking about death; she was gripped by anxiety attacks at all hours of the day, picturing herself dying from cancer in the next three months, imagining herself being run over by a car while out biking; she could hear the crackling of electricity in the walls, the buzzing of high-voltage power lines, she lived in fear of a short circuit that would burn down the house in the middle of the night; in her journal, she wrote that the feeling would most likely pass, that it was the incident in Valencia that was messing with her head, that she would never do anything stupid, that it would go as quickly as it had come, that it was best not to frighten her family and friends with her morbid thoughts, this too shall pass, she told herself over and over, *keep going, no feeling is final...*

... I was just as bad, I didn't say anything, didn't raise the alarm, it didn't matter how often my father would say that I was just a kid, that I didn't understand what was happening, I felt my mother slipping away from us bit by bit, I felt her melancholy penetrating my tender little girl's skin, but I didn't have the words to tell her any of this; sometimes, I'd surprise her while she was standing at the stove stirring a pot of soup, her eyes brimming with tears, sniffling discreetly...

It's just the onions, Laure.

I cut up a hot pepper and rubbed my eyes by accident.

Oh, it's nothing, I burned my hand putting something in the oven.

... I'm running toward the Valencia Bridge, toward the first of the aid stations, near the Veles e Vents building, I can see the four horizontal rectangles of the strange pavilion, I'll have to turn left soon, it's a shame the course doesn't run along the ocean, which is right nearby, I think about that picture of you running on a beach in the Caribbean, your form is perfect, you're gazing off into the distance, almost like nothing else exists but the movement of your body and the peaceful horizon...

KILOMETRE 4

... I spilled my drink all over myself, my tank top will dry, I look at my watch, so far, so good, I'm on pace, not tired, I'm breathing calmly, going with the flow, the picture of patience and determination,

the street is narrower here, the buildings create shade, I weave my way into a pack of focused runners, one of the men is breathing noisily in time with each stride, a gross-sounding wheeze that I won't be able to stand for much longer, we move forward, all characters in the same story, in the same corridor of air and asphalt, wearing down our soles layer by layer, engaging the same muscles, sweating under the same sun, suffering from the same thirst and exhaustion, aiming for the same horizon, a few palm trees here and there, the odd pastel facade, I take it all in, but my concentration is focused on my arms and legs, I let myself be carried along, I don't think about anything in particular, but I need to think about my mother, pay my respects, my mother, my mother, my mother and her motto, *running = calm*, she wrote it everywhere in her running journal, her entries would always start with a weather report...

Cloudy and humid today.

Ran to the mountain with M.

20 km and a bit.
We invented a new fartlek:
you speed up every time you pass another runner.
Oh my god, did we laugh.
No pain.
Just calm.

... I only just recently figured out what you meant, what the calm was that you were referring to; what I still can't figure out is why you were so desperate for that calm...

KILOMETRE 5

... my mouth is dry, thank god for aid stations and sugary drinks, now we're running past a fenced-in soccer field that feels never-ending, on my right I notice the tram tracks lying in an ochre bed on the ground, a long, slightly raised strip, I wonder if it's the tram line that leads to the Valencia Palace, another shiver runs down my spine,

I can't stand it when my skin crawls that way, maybe I should slow down a little... for a second, I catch a glimpse of the sea in the distance, then I'm forced to turn my back on the Mediterranean,

in a sudden flash, I see you screaming, your head pressed against the steering wheel, the moose on the snowy highway, like an apparition brought forth from the forest, I'll never forget your scream,

stay focused, the course veers off, hairpin turn, I

haven't seen the beach yet, I'm almost at aid station 5, tables on either side of the street, volunteers bust-ling about, pitchers in hand, others holding out paper cups, smiling, making eye contact, I grab one on the fly—¡ *Gracias* !—I pinch the rim together to stem the flow of the liquid, chug the contents in two or three gulps, bright orange drink, salty and citrusy in my throat, then toss the cup on the ground...

TRAVELLING LIGHT

Claire is balanced on a step stool, stretched out precariously on her tiptoes. She gropes around on the top shelf of her bedroom closet, pushing boxes out of the way, feeling around till her fingers land on the supple leather, which she grabs and pulls toward her. In a slithering motion, the bulky mauve purse slides off the shelf and onto her chest. Claire almost topples over.

She sits down on her unmade bed and stares coldly at the bag on her lap. Her eyelid twitches as she pulls open the silver zipper.

She dips her hand into the bag and pulls out what she initially thinks is a piece of raw meat, warm and smooth against her palm. Claire doesn't need to press her ear to the glistening mass to hear the pulsing sound that's getting louder, rising toward her, reverberating through the room like a ringing in the ears or the droning of a horsefly. A human heart. She examines it, recognizes arteries, aorta, vena cava, atria, dissected like on an anatomical diagram. The muscle quivers in her hand, pumping and circulating an increasingly large amount of blood, which soon overflows her cupped palms, runs down her forearms, and soaks her skin, the purse, and the pearl grey sheets under her thighs.

In the hallway, Laure is pounding on the door, rattling the doorknob, yelling at the top of her lungs. "Mama! Maaamaaa!"

As Claire goes to shove the heart back in the bag, it begins to swell, a gelatinous blob that takes on size, that she can barely contain. She lets out a scream when the heart slips between her fingers and flops to the bedroom floor.

"Mama! Mama! Get up! There's blood all over the floor. Léon's nose is bleeding again. And he used up all the milk for his cereal..."

WHEN TO LEAVE?

"Jean, I need a vacation," Claire declares a few hours later, her fingers gripped tightly around the phone receiver. "I really need a change of scenery. I'd like you to watch the kids for ten days."

They're both silent for a beat.

"Um, and you're going where, and with—"

Claire cuts him off. "None of your business, Jean. I need some time to clear my head."

A longer silence this time. Jean doesn't understand, starts to protest.

"It's a bad idea. If I were you, I'd—"

"I'm not asking for your opinion, Jean. I'm telling you that I'm leaving."

"Just like that? Without consulting me? So, what? I should just say *bon voyage*, off you go, have a great time?"

Claire raises her voice.

"Seriously? And what about all your diving trips, your Venice Biennales, your weekends in New York City with your architect buddies, your week-long hunting trips up north?"

"Don't start with that again, Claire. I've never held you back, I even encouraged you to go back to work, take on new jobs. Shit, enough's enough. Maybe it's time you get over the whole thing, you didn't even know the wom—"

Claire slams the receiver down. But she continues the conversation, raging at the kitchen wall.

"Enough, Jean! Don't you dare tell me how I should feel, you didn't even goddamn care enough to hug me, you did fuck all to comfort me after she killed herself right in front of me, you piece of..."

She pounds her fist against the door frame. Blood vessels burst under her skin. Behind her, a purple painted cat hanging on the end of a nail wobbles, and Claire hears it crash to the floor. Pieces of broken glass scatter in all directions, some disappearing under the stove. Claire examines the edge of her palm; the skin is turning red, like an instant sunburn or the kind of embarrassing injury you'd get if you were stupid enough to stick your hand into a flaming toaster.

She grinds her molars together—two hundred pounds of pressure per square inch, her dentist reminds her at each checkup. When she finally unclenches her jaw, a pool of frothy saliva leaks out and a string of drool runs down her chin and falls to the slate floor. Three drops of rage among the shards of glass at her feet.

AT THE AIRPORT

The city has been in the grips of a heatwave for three days—five people dead already—and it's early August 2015 when Claire sets her suitcase down on the conveyor belt at the American Airlines check-in counter. It's been a long time since she's wandered around an airport alone. In the air-conditioned climate of the Montreal airport, she fans the top of her dress to dry the sweat trickling down her back and between her breasts. She makes her way to the duty-free shop, where she spots a bottle of limited-edition Absolut Honey vodka with the message *Honey, I'm coming home* emblazoned on the bottle in stylized letters. She pictures a smiling woman paying for the alcohol and carrying it onto the plane, happy to be heading home to her sweetheart. Claire frowns and instead buys a bottle of microdistilled gin with a large parsnip on the bottle.

She orders a coffee, watches the news distractedly: seventy-one bodies found in a refrigerated truck left on the side of a highway in Austria, near the Hungarian border. Fifty-nine men, eight women and four children. It's more of an uneasy feeling than an actual image that forms in her head. It's hard to imagine a pile of corpses: exposed necks, dark hair, sagging backs, legs splayed open, arms crossed over motionless chests. Her brain conjures up a formless heap, like in a mass grave, then quickly switches channels, unable to reconcile the mental picture with the humanity of each of the refugees decomposing in the truck, which was previously owned by a Slovakian poultry company and which the traffickers bought, registered in Romania, then abandoned on the highway.

On the plane, she can hear babies crying—you can't not hear them, their symphony of cries starts up well before takeoff. Those years are behind her. No more pacing up and down the aisles with a baby screaming in her ears. She noticed them earlier, standing at gate A50, the stressed-out wives and mothers with their anxious expressions, always on the alert, unable to relax. They never sit down, they stay standing the whole time, waiting for the boarding call, keeping an eye on the kids, criticizing the husband, sighing with exasperation. The fear of the delayed flight, the interminably long lineup, the impossibly heavy suitcase, the hyperactive child: They're focused only on what could go wrong.

TRAVELLING FOR A LIVING

In her late teens, Claire had devoured the *Work Your Way Around the World* guide and piles of *Lonely Planet*, *Guides du routard* and *Rough Guides* travel books. She'd dreamed about writing guidebooks and had eventually wound up being paid to take part in organized tours, getaways, journeys, treks, expeditions and all sorts of off-the-beaten-path adventures.

The years had passed, and Claire Halde had racked up passport stamps and published articles like so many victories and milestones on her personal journey toward becoming the woman who'd aspired to travel, write and, above all, feel free. But the trips weren't like they used to be. Comfort levels had changed, and the tourists were changing too, as communications and connections—by land and sea, even in far-flung locations—became more frequent and better adapted to the obsessive Western quest for a change of scenery. As people began travelling more and all over the world, so Claire felt less inclined to help them on their way.

She'd worked breaks into her travel itineraries, coming home at regular intervals. But, over the years and with the arrival of the kids, her enthusiasm had waned, and the wind had gone out of her sails. It didn't bother her anymore to stay in port, to postpone her departures. The whole thing had lost its appeal, its charm, its novelty.

She'd told her editors that she just wasn't into it anymore, that she'd prefer to work at a desk than in the field, and that, no, she would not update a "tiny little" section of the upcoming new edition of *Three Days in Valencia* just because she "happened" to be on vacation in Spain.

Yet, it's what she'd pictured herself doing for the rest of her life. At twenty-five, fresh out of university, it had been easy to imagine that travelling and writing would be enough, that they'd fill up her days, that hopes and ambitions would be sufficiently satisfied to call it a life, a life deliberately chosen and lived to the fullest.

It had been her roadmap.

LANDING IN SPAIN

Waiting at the luggage carrousel at Barcelona's El Prat Airport, Claire stifles an exhausted yawn. She refuses to let her impatience and irritation show, refuses to pounce on every black, rectangular suitcase that looks like every other black, rectangular suitcase. Claire Halde remains stock-still, impassive, a little nostalgic for the years when she used to travel with nothing but a carry-on backpack. Standing in the middle of the bustling crowd, she downs the last few sips of her stale mineral water. *So much for sparkling.*

THINGS SEEN AND DONE

It's fair to say that Claire Halde had travelled in her life. Since her first plane ticket—a return trip bought at the age of fifteen with the money she'd earned slaving away at her dishwashing job, spending every weekend up to her elbows in tepid water, rinsing greasy smears off stemware, washing fingerprints and lip marks off delicate goblets, scraping bland Neapolitan sauce and congealed cheese off plates at a tourist-trap trattoria in the Old Port—she'd seen a place or two.

In the cities, she'd admired the worn stones of the cathedrals and the crumbling castles, never tiring of exploring temples or touring air-conditioned museums on days when the sweltering heat drove her indoors. She'd strolled casually through gardens and parks, where she'd picnicked, watched the pigeons and ducks, dodged aggressive monkeys roaming freely and dogs left off their leashes. She'd sat on wooden or concrete benches, under trees in full bloom.

She'd gotten lost in medieval streets, explored boulevards crammed with boutiques and tourists, where she'd window-shopped or bargained fiercely, always watching her step, avoiding the dog turds during the day and the giant cockroaches at night. She'd photographed panoramic vistas and bodies of water, countless ruins and architectural marvels, colourful facades, and faces that she'd found particularly inspiring, haggard, fresh or photogenic.

She'd often ventured outside the cities to camp beneath the stars, meander through rice paddies, sail rivers and lakes in makeshift boats, cross deserts and canyons by train, spend bone-jarring nights on long bus rides, soar in planes and helicopters over four different oceans and the lands above the clouds, always attuned to the time zone, attentive to the movement of the hands on her watch, turning the tiny dial forward or backward between her thumb and index finger. She'd trekked through forests, snapping dead branches under her bulky Gore-Tex boots and jumping at the faintest sound on the trails, and she'd scaled mountains and volcanoes, barely flinching as she picked her way along the sheer rocky paths.

Holding her breath, she'd swum through murky and crystal-clear waters alike; she'd forded rivers, water up to her neck, backpack balanced on her head, skin covered in leeches, which were later burned off with the lit tip of a cigarette. She'd asked strangers for directions, hailed taxis and tuk-tuks, hitchhiked on desolate highways in Borneo, Argentina, Mexico, Pakistan, Moldova, and her own province. She'd shared the padded bench of an eighteen-wheeler with a Kiwi travel companion, her ass planted on the hot, sticky leather next to a trucker on his first experience picking up hitchhikers. The same bench that they'd reclined come nightfall, somewhere between Singapore and Kuala Lumpur, when the driver had pulled off into the parking lot of a big-box supermarket: *We sleep here tonight.* She'd closed her eyes, placing her trust all night long in the trucker, who had trusted her in return; no one had robbed anyone or touched anyone inappropriately, and in the morning they'd woken up to the glorious sound of birds singing in the trees, before hitting the road again.

GETTING AROUND BARCELONA

After arriving in the Catalan capital, Claire wades into the August heat; it's early afternoon and the last patrons are making their way off the patios, restaurant owners are pulling down their steel grates, people are sluggish from too much meat, wine and dessert, full up with small talk. The sidewalks are sizzling, and the air is heavy with humidity. Claire's feet are dragging, and her shoulder is aching from pulling her bag awkwardly behind her. Her fingers grip the sticky handle of the rolling suitcase, a medium-sized receptacle that holds everything she'll need for her trip. Dresses and paperbacks, shampoo and sandals, a few running outfits, a bathing suit, sunscreen, a light sweater for the cool evenings. Every now and then, the case bumps over a stray pebble, a crack in the sidewalk or an uneven paving stone and teeters like a woman who's had too much to drink.

She has an appointment at three o'clock to pick up the keys for a tiny room she's booked through Airbnb. She's hungry and tired, already tired, and the trip is just getting started.

WHERE TO SLEEP?

Claire had laid the full weight of her eyelids on hundreds of pillows in her years as a traveller. Between sheets worn thin by other bodies, she'd woken up to the sound of the muezzin calling the believers to prayer, the cacophony of howler monkeys, the strident wake-up calls of roosters, the admonishments of mothers scolding their brood. Her memory had eventually dimmed on the string of nights and rooms, the exact moments of drifting off and waking up, and even the dreams—the succession of chills, nightmares and sweats in borrowed beds. Only vague impressions remained of laundromat smells, damp, creased cotton, springs creaking and insects scuttling about in cheap rooms, rough woollen blankets rasping in sleeper cars. But she clearly remembered the obese rats scurrying in the ceiling, the throat-clearing, coughing and spitting in the adjacent rooms, sometimes accompanied by shameless cries of ecstasy, and she could still see the white mice darting past her feet, their red eyes gleaming, gnawing at the walls and leaving piles of droppings behind in the dresser drawers.

During her nights plagued by insomnia, she'd been hyper-aware of the slightest sounds: the gurgling of the radiator, the whirling of the fan, the creaking of a door in the hallway, the breathing of travel companions with whom she'd shared rooms, beds, or ships' cabins on long ocean crossings. Yes, for years, Claire Halde had preferred changes of scenery to life in one place.

WHERE TO EAT?

The metal implements click against the porcelain, blade slicing back and forth, fork spearing a pea. Staring across the checkered tablecloth at the empty chair across from her, Claire spins the delicate teaspoon counterclockwise, an idle movement designed to kill time. Her neighbour to the left is doing the same thing, sawing away with knife and fork at a particularly sinewy bit—seems the stew on the menu of the day wasn't such a great choice, after all. He dips his knife into the dainty butter dish, tears apart a roll in a shower of crumbs, and butters his bread meticulously. His chewing is ill-mannered, his bites man-sized, clearly the appetite of a guy who's worked all his life, who earns a living from 9 a.m. to 1 p.m., then again from 2 p.m. to 6 p.m. He checks his watch often and looks at Claire only once, out of the corner of his eye; he smiles vaguely and turns his attention back to his flan, jabbing it repeatedly with his spoon, polishing it off in four bites. He raises his hand to call for a coffee, then to summon the bill. Claire is still stretching out her dessert, a berry sorbet, which she nibbles through pursed lips, like someone who's not crazy about cold food or fruit. Time passes in a succession of tiny bites, and the sorbet melts. After all that, it's almost 3 p.m.

NOT TO BE MISSED:
CULINARY DELICACIES

During her travels, Claire Halde had sampled a variety of foods with either curiosity or indifference: exotic fruits; traditional dishes; bland, pasty gruels; local sweets; Turkish delights that had stuck to the roof of her mouth in the streets of Istanbul; assorted confections; Italian ices; and myriad varieties of rice, kasha, flatbreads, fried breads and soft breads. In the port city of one of the Maluku Islands, she'd savoured a pineapple that she'd never forget, its juices running down her wrist while she waited for a cargo ship that was taking its sweet time docking. On the Trans-Siberian Railway, she'd drunk countless cups of tea and eaten a pot of rhubarb jam (a gift for the train ride to the Urals) with a tiny spoon. In Warsaw, she'd downed her first-ever cup of coffee, a bitter Turkish brew, in one gulp. Somewhere in the middle of the Indian Ocean, she'd been laid flat by seasickness, puking up her meal over the railing: salty noodles in a greasy broth, the lone menu item on the Ambon-Surabaya crossing. And again, years later, head pounding and pinned to her bed in the middle of a storm on an expedition through the Patagonian fjords, she'd choked down her bile only to spew it up again into a coffee mug that had quickly overflowed, all the while trying to fix her eyes and plant her hands on something—anything—that wasn't already pitching and heaving in the ship's cabin, which wouldn't stop spinning.

She'd tied one on more than once on the road, relishing the burning sensation of the vodka, arak and rum, mixed with fresh juices and luscious fruits plucked straight from the tree: mangoes, rambutans, mangosteens and others whose names she'll never know. Then there had been the warm milk, manioc, breakfasts of fish and boiled callaloo, seafood soups in the Valparaíso market at night and, in the markets of Asia, bowls of fragrant, steaming broth floating with chunks of mystery meat and strange-tasting balls that looked suspiciously like animal testicles. What else? Thali eaten off banana leaves, staining fingernails yellow with turmeric. Small packets of sticky rice wrapped up like trinkets bought from old ladies in train stations. Green almonds picked in a garden in Santiago. Curries and peppers hot enough to make her eyes water. The unforgettable flavours of her journeys, like a travelogue engraved on her taste buds.

BARCELONA ON A SHOESTRING

Her room is in a quaint building at the end of a sloped, flower-lined alley. Assorted cacti stand in pots next to the front door, which gives onto a gloomy stairwell. Claire hauls her suitcase up to the third floor.

Her hosts greet her warmly, show her around the room, hand her a set of keys, give her the wi-fi password and explain how the gas stove and shower work.

Claire sits down on the narrow bed, suddenly overwhelmed by an exhaustion that runs deeper than just the regular sluggishness of jet lag. The room is so cramped that the single bed barely fits into the space along the wall, to the left of the door. She has to slide her suitcase under the bed to make room to move around. A tiny window looks out onto the neighbours' patio. The place is lacking in charm, but Claire tells herself that it'll do. *It's only somewhere to sleep, to rest for a while before heading back to Valencia.*

She stretches out, smooths the wrinkles from her dress, searches for a pen in her bag. On the back of her boarding pass, she jots down a few reminders before they slip her mind:

Buy train ticket

Book room at Valencia Palace

Run → Parc de les Aigües or beach

(map out 25–30 km)

~~Go back to Sagrada Família~~

Find address of place they keep unclaimed bodies

Buy postcards for kids

Hairdresser?

KILOMETRE 6

... a slight incline, no sweat, *the fastest marathon in Spain,* I chose well for my first marathon, no hills, elevation that doesn't aggravate my calf injury, the shooting pain that developed this summer after my hill sprint workouts, there's the campus on my right, the road's widening out here, finally some room to breathe, some people have already slowed down, quick glance at my watch,

all good, five minutes thirty-eight seconds per kilometre, sidelong glance at the gardens planted down the middle of Avenida de Blasco Ibáñez: neatly trimmed shrubbery, hedges and gravel, leafy trees, a fountain,

it's November and everything's still green, it's pretty, I'd pictured the city as being shabbier, dirtier, from reading your journals, I'd never have guessed that Valencia was so beautiful, back then you were living under what Dad called a "black cloud," always seeing the glass as half empty, it took a while for your friends and family to realize, to admit that it wasn't just a passing phase, you were never the same after Valencia, but what they couldn't know is that after that trip to Spain, a part of you—the sweet, sunny part—would never quite make it back...

KILOMETRE 7

... I'm trailing behind a man, fortyish I'd say, the word *Guide* printed on his back, he's attached at the wrist to a woman wearing an orange vest emblazoned with *Blind* in black letters, people are applauding her and cheering her on, a chill runs down my spine, I grin, see what you're missing, Mama, we could be here together running in Valencia, together like these two, mother and daughter, side by side, crossing one of your fifti-eth-birthday wishes off the list... I wonder what the point is of running without being able to see what's in front of you, how it feels to depend so completely on someone else, to experience the movements, sounds and smells without any outside interference, to move about in the dark and match your pace to someone else's, maybe they're a couple, I speed up slightly to pass them, I need quiet so I can focus, I can't stand shouting and displays of emotion, they make me uncomfortable, like hugs, I look at my watch, I've been running for about half an hour, not very long, but it went by fast, I do the math: one-sixth of the course, one-third of a half-marathon, still three hundred metres to go before kilometre seven, seven kilometres, that's a round trip

between my apartment and the architecture department, I've done that run hundreds of times...

KILOMETRE 8

... I'm entering my comfort zone now, forty minutes,
that's how long it takes to get to that state where I lose
all sense of myself, a second wind, a different kind
of effort, a mild floating sensation, like a cushion of
air under my feet, I feel powerful and free, I notice
smells, sounds and the quality of the light, for a second
I register the faces of the people in the crowds, I high-
five the kids, I finger the energy gel in my pocket, won't
be long now, can't miss the next water station, must tear
open the pouch before I reach the tables, that's my biggest fear—collapsing because I miscalculated my fluids
and carbs, I hate it when I can feel my body starting to
weaken, when the little stars appear in front of my eyes
and the back of my neck starts to tingle, I remember that
day, not long after we got back from Spain, when you
went for a run in the country, it was a Sunday and it was
really hot out, it was the first time you'd gone for such
a long run, three hours just a few weeks out from your
first marathon, we'd waited to have supper with you,
the noodles had all clumped together in the strainer,
Dad was getting impatient and was about to go looking
for you in the car, Léon had started crying because he
was hungry and scared that you'd been attacked by a

bear that had wandered out of the forest, we'd just sat down at the table and started eating without you when you staggered in, dripping with sweat, I remember Dad yelling: Where were you? We've been waiting an hour for you. The pasta's cold.

... you'd run out of water, started to feel sick, sunstroke or mild dehydration had forced you to stop a number of times, you'd mumbled an apology, then shut yourself in the bathroom, we could hear you crying, we couldn't ignore your sobs as we chewed and swallowed our spaghetti, clutching onto the door frame, you'd screamed: I just ran for three hours! I just ran for three hours and all you can say is, the pasta is cold?

... I don't have many memories of you and Dad together, but I've never forgotten that one, I can still picture you: you're wearing a turquoise tank top and your face is crumpled with exhaustion, your hair is soaked with sweat and your forehead is flushed with anger and resentment, you're sitting on the edge of the bathtub crying, and there's Dad, walking away from you, into the kitchen to put away the dishes, clattering the plates together...

KILOMETRE 9

... I push my earbuds further into my ears, I didn't want music at first, but now that I've hit my stride, I press shuffle:

One way or another, I'm gonna find ya

... I'm starting to wonder if this sappiness was such a good idea, I'd thought it was only fitting to add a few of your favourites to my playlist, to include the music that had kept you moving during your marathons, I'd thought it might make you feel a little closer, but suddenly, I'm not so sure, I'm afraid it'll bum me out and slow me down instead, when Dad gave me your journals, he'd said: they'll help you understand a few things about your mother, and about me too, things you might wish you'd never known, but actually they don't explain anything, some things simply defy explanation: one day, people are there with you and you love each other, and then something breaks and they're not there anymore, they're somewhere else, it's cruel and you don't know why, but that's just the way it is, and the sooner you understand that, the better off you are...

KILOMETRE 10

... I shove two gumdrops in my mouth, lemonade flavour, chew, chew, chew, my mouth is a little dry, the sweet jelly sticks to my teeth, I'd kill for a glass of water, I notice a woman with brown hair leaning against a barrier on the side of the road, she smiles at me warmly, nods her head and gives me two thumbs up,

It was me on that road
But you couldn't see me

Too many lights out, but nowhere near here
It was me on that road
Still you couldn't see me

... for a second, I wonder if I'd recognize my mother if she were actually there, hidden among the crowd, watching the runners go by as though nothing were out of the ordinary...

Road's end getting nearer
We cover distance but not together

... I speed up as I run through the ten-kilometre arch, I watch the numbers scroll by, hear the drums, see the banners, for a brief moment my lungs feel like they're on fire...

It's about you and the sun
A morning run

... fifty-six minutes thirty-four seconds, I'm on pace...

THE TIME DIFFERENCE

The morning after a sleepless night in the Central European Time zone (UTC+1), Claire has trouble getting out of bed, but she's intent on getting in a run before the midday heat, determined to stick to her Sunday schedule: two hours and thirty minutes, almost three hours of basic endurance training through the city streets. Just before 10 a.m., she sets out along Avinguda Diagonal, toward the sea, her legs on autopilot, her mind momentarily blank, her only ailment some mild stiffness around her collarbones, and already the sun is beating down.

LEAVING BARCELONA

Claire Halde spends a restless last night in her narrow bed in Barcelona. Her leg muscles are aching, and the room is sticky, a combination of the mercury topping out at over thirty degrees Celsius and the total lack of ventilation. The humidity is brutal; nothing she does takes her mind off it. She dreams about the woman in Valencia, hears her hoarse voice in her nightmare. She wakes up often. Still suffering from jet lag, she's worried she'll oversleep and miss her train to Valencia.

But she doesn't. A few hours later, Tarragona flashes past the window of compartment 5. Claire gazes at the passing landscape absently: green hills, huge oil refineries like the ones on the outskirts of all big cities, parched fields, unkempt grass, a layer of dust floating above the brown earth. She registers it all through a narrow slit, eyelids drooping heavily in a state of half-sleep.

TRAVEL BY TRAIN

When she wakes up, nothing about the view has changed; it's still the same monotonous, forward progression, the same flat, white sky and tall, yellow grass, the same stiff blue seats and paper headrest covers with the Renfe logo, the same hypnotic rolling motion along the railroad tracks, and the same passengers roaming up and down the aisles. It's early afternoon in August, six years after the encounter on the roof, and the train will be pulling into the station momentarily.

When it comes to the sea and the beach in Valencia, Claire Halde remembers them as being completely grey, a remarkably dreary landscape scoured by a wind that numbs all feeling. Valencia is blanketed by a thick layer of fog. Claire can't help but be reminded of the scene in the Antonioni film *Red Desert*, where the ship is quarantined in the misty port, and the characters are all standing some distance apart from each other, silent and still, as the fog rolls in between them on the dock, gradually engulfing them until they are swallowed up completely. Even though she knows full well that the movie is set in Italy, Claire overlaps the two different moods and lights, jumbles the sets, confuses the halftones. In her memories of Valencia, her hair is thick and lush, and it's plastered to her face exactly like the actress in the movie when the wind blows. And there's the same sadness in her eyes, the same sombre expression; her face is etched with a heavy weariness. In her mind's eye, she's Monica Vitti, staring off into the sky, gazing out over the sea in Valencia on a day that's windy and grey, utterly grey, the light too weak to penetrate the dense fog that hangs over the shore. For Claire Halde, the Valencian seaside will forever be enveloped in a cinematic mist.

KILOMETRE 11

... I'm not the type to commune with a city while I'm running, the monuments elude me, the trees blend into the background, I forge ahead along straight lines and around bends, from time to time picking out a face, a waving hand, a child's smile, a vista of a park or a boulevard, a bridge up ahead, it's like I'm running through Valencia without actually seeing anything, blankly scanning everything in my path—buildings and intersections, people walking, striding, standing still, pavement and scraps of sky the odd time I decide to look up—I focus on nothing except moving forward and my determination to not quit, not slow down, not quit, not end up on a stretcher, I know what it is I don't want to find in Valencia, but I'm not exactly sure what it is I came looking for,

maybe I'll figure it out tomorrow, when my muscles are tired and aching, maybe I'll feel defenceless and exposed the day after this marathon and maybe that's what it'll take for me to fully absorb Valencia; I've felt tense and nervous ever since I got here, I blamed the marathon and my fear of missing the start time or my legs giving out on me or my stomach acting up, I put it down to my fear of failing and getting injured and disappointing everyone back home in Montreal glued to their screens, tracking my progress, watching the clock and the kilometre markers tick by, but I also know that my stiffness stems from something more insidious, a deep-seated fear—I don't want to come back from Valencia with a belly full of my mother's misery...

KILOMETRE 12

... at first, I'd talk to you non-stop in my head, a secret dialogue, a daydream in which you were very much alive, I'd become hopelessly tangled up in sentences that I'd analyze endlessly to myself, I was somewhere else entirely, I have no idea now why I had so much to say to you, at an age when the last person kids want to talk to is their mother, but not me, I was constantly drawn back to that conversation in my brain, I'd fill you in on my days at school or what I ate, but other times our talks were more serious, about my disappointments, my heartbreaks, my unrequited loves, then, as time went by, the exchanges fizzled out, that was no way to spend my teen years...

... our conversation struck up again when I took up running, I started talking to the runner you once were, to the woman I'd have liked at my side, for all those kilometres that we couldn't run together; it's a more resigned sort of conversation now, I'd have liked to have a mother who was bright and present, a mother without any cracks, not an *unreal mother* floating in a ray of light, set for all eternity against an autumn backdrop, face frozen in a mysterious expression...

KILOMETRE 13

... almost one-quarter, no, one-third down, and each step brings me closer to the finish line, I run straight ahead, no zigzagging, following the white line painted on the ground, so far, so good, *relax your shoulders*, I think I need to pee, but I don't want to stop, don't think about it, it'll pass...

... this too shall pass, you used to say to me, Mama, when I was upset as a kid, and then there was that verse by Rilke that you'd pinned up over your desk: "Let everything happen to you: beauty and terror. Just keep going. No feeling is final."

... beauty and terror, that moose on the deserted, snow-covered highway, blood flowing from its flank, majestic, eyes moist, an enormous creature materialized from the forest, the screeching of the brakes, the violent lurch of our bodies and the miracle, the car skidding and coming to a stop mere inches from the animal, which took off at a gallop, leaving a trail of blood behind it in the snow, its antlers wider than a child lying on its side, and you, screaming in terror, pounding your forehead against the steering wheel, and me, so small in my car seat, reassuring you: But he's not dead, Mama, we're not dead, it's okay, you didn't kill him...

KILOMETRE 14

... when I'm running, I allow myself to surrender to the movement, to my linear progression through space, like now, everything's on track, I'm experiencing a moment of lightness, a momentum that carries me over the border between within and without, between my head and the street, my radar is attuned to all the bumps in the road, to the puddles and the cracks, the broken glass and the dog shit, I let my mind wander, from my love of running to the aches and pains in my joints and everything in between, my worries have been pushed to the back of my mind, a sense of calm settles in, bit by bit, step by step, I refocus on the scenery, on the trees and the storefronts, on what's going on around me, then on what's going on inside me, I turn inwards, to the burning in my lungs, the beating of my heart, the wandering thoughts, and the air that's travelling in and out, in and out, my breathing becoming increasingly laboured as I pick up the pace, maintain the rhythm, give in to the fatigue,

I bend the surfaces to my will, my feet are used to the snow and the mud, the hardness of the concrete that jars my legs, but I'm wary of the paving stones here, the ancient and uneven slabs, I talk myself through it, never losing focus, the excitement in the city is intoxicating, the sound of drums pounding here, people crowding into the intersection further along, I duck into the shadow of a building, on the shady side of the street, I slip into the sensible horizon...

KILOMETRE 15

Love me, love me, love me, say you do

... I can't believe my mother would run to such a slow song...

Let me fly away with you

... I've been running past it for almost a kilometre now, but I can't remember the name of this park, the one with the museum of nature, the green lungs of Valencia...

Run, sweetheart, run! You can do it!

... I'm running, Mama, I'm running, see how I'm running, I'm not thinking about love, I'm just running, and there's no one waiting for me at the finish line...

GETTING ORIENTED IN VALENCIA

In Valencia, Claire Halde doesn't recognize the train station. It's like she's never been to the city before, she can't get her bearings, she has no idea where she is in relation to the hotel. She has to ask directions from a transit company employee, an irascible man with a bushy moustache who eventually hands her a map of the system.

The instant she steps off the N3 bus with her rolling suitcase, her gaze is drawn to the spot where the woman jumped from. The Valencia Palace Hotel is right there, looming large in front of her. The bushes are fuller, and the plants on the rooftop terrace around the pool have grown taller. She walks toward the building, locking eyes on the fourth floor, then on the sidewalk below, mentally calculating the drop between the two. She feels numb—a combination of exhaustion from the trip, the heat and hunger pangs. It's almost 2 p.m., and the mercury reads thirty-five degrees, she's had barely anything to eat, her dress is sticking to her back, and her hair is frizzing at the nape of her neck. She squares her shoulders and walks into the Valencia Palace.

STAYING IN VALENCIA:
THE VALENCIA PALACE HOTEL

At the front desk, she's given a key card for room 1402, where she sets down her case, draws back the curtains, looks out the window at everything happening below: cars driving through the roundabout, taxis pulling up, doors opening and closing, smoke rising from a distant chimney, and a Leroy Merlin warehouse store, rectangular and white, sitting next to a highway.

Claire ventures out to pick up some ham and manchego, yellow-fleshed plums, mineral water and a hazelnut chocolate bar. After the grocery store, she walks over to Benicalap Park, quiet this early in the afternoon. Next to a dry fountain streaked with pigeon droppings, which stand out in stark contrast to the absinthe-green cast iron and rusty spouts, she eats alone, feeling a little unsettled, glancing over her shoulder repeatedly like someone might be spying on her. She doesn't linger, she scoffs down her meal, eager to be finished.

OFF THE BEATEN PATH:
BENICALAP PARK

Skirting the edge of Benicalap Park, she has no trouble finding the overgrown lot again. The abandoned building is still standing, but it's in shambles. Probably squatter central. She notices two officers—a man and a woman—inspecting the premises. They're dressed in uniform with fluorescent stripes on their arms, most likely cops walking the beat. The female officer is waving her hand in front of her nose, as though trying to shoo away a stubborn fly, a lingering stench or the smell of death. Maybe they've found a body. Or a dead animal, at the very least. Or maybe someone took a shit right out in the open and now it's baking in the sun. She should have just gone back to the hotel, grabbed her stuff and headed out to the tourist area, where geraniums bloom prettily in pots on window ledges. Claire has no desire to be asked what she's doing here, spying on the cops at work. And to think she walked through here with her kids, barely an hour after the suicide.

GETTING AROUND VALENCIA

With her index finger, Claire Halde traces the canary yellow line to a transfer station, where it turns into a red line that runs to the Xàtiva stop. She stuffs the tourist map into the side pocket of her bag, which already contains a tattered map of the Barcelona metro system, a pamphlet for an exhibition on the avant-gardists, and a jumble of fortune cookie sayings collected over the span of months. It was a terrible obsession, hoarding all those scraps of paper—brochures, free itineraries and maps from tourist offices, hotel receipts, metro tickets, train tickets, boarding passes—which she'd cart home from her travels and then couldn't bring herself to part with. She'd developed the habit back when she was writing travel guides for the *Discovery* series. Whenever she'd get home from another trip, she'd tuck the pile of papers, crumpled from being haphazardly folded, unfolded and refolded, into plastic sleeves, which she'd label in marker "Spain 2009," for example. She told herself she'd go through them one day, the evidence of her travels and all the time she'd spent abroad. But she never touched them again.

KILOMETRE 16

... already fifteen kilometres down, feeling great, we're near the Río again, I know that white bridge over there, the La Peineta Bridge over the Turia gardens, the one designed by Calatrava, it reminds me of the one near the Guggenheim in Bilbao, of that picture of me and my mother, the one where I'm crouched at her feet, utterly fascinated by the glass tiles under us, I'd thought about carrying a picture of you, but I was worried it would get all crumpled and faded, which would only end up depressing me, so instead I fastened the safety pins from the race bib you wore during your last marathon against my breast, that's all I could find in the way of a good luck charm, a few rusty pins...

KILOMETRE 17

... for the past little while, I've felt light, like a sixty-kilo-gram gust of air, bodiless but at the same time deeply rooted, I glide, skin against wind, leaping, landing, taking off again, like nothing can stop me, not pain or exhaustion, the city is my oyster, I'm not intimidated by the distance, I'm no longer afraid, momentum is a powerful thing, I'm a body in motion, in my mind's eye I'm seeing a slideshow of all the pictures I've looked at so often: my mother, looking cool in her apple-green sweater, one elbow resting on the handle of my stroller, striking a pose next to a fountain in Grenada, legs crossed, hip cocked, stray locks framing her face, she's holding my hand and smiling down at me, my dad took the picture; my mother, hugely pregnant in the garden, a few days before my brother was born, a magnolia tree in full bloom behind her, I'm kissing her belly, chubby in my ruffled dress, dimple in my cheek, nose pressed up against the taut skin of her stomach, she's wearing sunglasses and her pink lips are formed into a mysterious half-smile...

KILOMETRE 18

Watch your posture, Laure. Stand up straight, Laure.
    ... I straighten up, an imaginary steel wire pulling my head straight up toward the sky, I picture my mother cracking her neck, my mother and her migraines, her neck muscles so often pinched, when I was little she'd ask me to massage her temples and I'd oblige with my tiny hands, she'd often lie on her stomach and tell me

to write something on her back, I remember spending hours on the couch, long winter afternoons sliding my fingers under her cashmere sweaters, into her warmth, she was always so good at figuring out what I was spelling on her skin, often guessing the word after the second or third letter, yelling out Cat! Flower! I love you! Poop!

... when it was my turn to guess, you'd write long, complicated words and I'd ask you to start over again and again, just so I could savour the feeling of you tickling my back for a little while longer...

KILOMETRE 19

... we're doubling back now on the Blasco Ibáñez stretch from earlier, passing the last runners headed the other way, they're only on kilometre 9, there's that determined lady who already looks like she's in trouble, and that skinny old man still shuffling along, he must be about eighty...

Stay strong, Laure. Don't slow down, keep going, you can do it.

KILOMETRE 20

I was looking for you, are you gone gone?
Called you on the phone, another dimension.
Well, you never returned, oh you know what I mean.

I went looking for you, are you gone gone?

... huge apartment buildings, so much boring, brown stucco, they seriously need to plant some trees around here...

Down by the ocean it was so dismal,
Women all standing with a shock on their faces.
Sad description, oh I was looking for you.

... I think the beach is at the end of this street where the tram goes, we're running toward the sea, but we never actually see it, the sweat is trickling down my temples, I'm trying not to think about how hot it'll be at noon, now that the sun's out...

Picked up my key, didn't reply.
Went to my room, started to cry.
You were small, an angel, are you gone gone?

... the air is heavy and suffocating, not at all fresh, grey and scorching hot, and that annoying sun, melting my resolve, *down by the ocean it was so dismal*, I wonder what *dismal* means...

You'll never return into my arms 'cause you were gone gone.

Never return into my arms 'cause you were gone gone.
Gone gone, gone gone, goodbye.

NOT TO BE MISSED:
PUERTA DE SERRANOS

Cutting through the back streets of Ciutat Vella, trailing other pedestrians who seem to have a better idea of where they're going, Claire ambles toward the Puerta de Serranos. She walks in without paying and climbs to the top of the tower that she wasn't brave enough to visit six years earlier. At the top, she tries to pick out the Valencia Palace Hotel in the distance but can't find it. Suddenly, her head starts spinning. Her legs go weak; looking down at the street below, she thinks: The woman could have jumped from here. There's nothing stopping anyone from straddling the thick wall punctuated with crenellations and arrow slits. It would be so easy to throw yourself off the top of this tower, if you felt so inclined. She imagines the splintering sound the bones would make, the dizzying free-fall followed by the impact with the pavement, the screams of the tourists. It's a mental image that she's powerless to resist. Like an itchy scab that's not quite healed, she thinks, and the satisfaction you get from scratching around the edges, lifting it up with a fingernail, then ripping it off completely.

She descends the stairs on legs as nebulous as smoke, picking her way down the five-hundred-year-old steps like she was walking through water, haunted by the terrifying, stomach-lurching vision of the fall the whole way down. Her attraction to the void is just one of the obsessions she's been battling since childhood, on top of her bizarre impulse to stick a needle in her eye and her disturbing compulsion to jump onto the metro tracks or throw herself out of a speeding car while riding shotgun down a highway.

WHERE TO SLEEP?

She'd booked a room at the Valencia Palace for the first three nights. For the rest of her stay, she'd created an account on couchsurfing.com at the last minute, to prove to herself that she was still capable of handling the unknown, of travelling like she did in her twenties, of going with the flow, of sleeping anywhere. For her profile, she'd picked a Slavic-sounding first name, chosen a good picture of herself—sparkling eyes and mysterious half-smile—filled out the questionnaire conservatively, emphasizing her extensive travels, areas of interest and flawless Spanish.

During her travels, Claire had let many a toothless old man take her in his arms. Mothers had pinched her cheeks with squeals of delight, handing over their bare-bottomed babies for her to dandle on her knee during interminable and inconvenient connections. In the capital cities of southeast Asia, in two-dollar-a-night guest houses—windowless rooms, mattresses on the floor reeking of pest repellant, ceiling fans spinning lazily—she'd shared quarters with heroin addicts and prostitutes, smiling at them without making eye contact. At nineteen, she'd promised herself she'd never end up like them, even as she feared she'd never be able to keep that promise.

She sometimes thinks about other travellers she's crossed paths with over the years. Some had come on to her, inviting her to cross North America with them on the back of their motorbike, others had made love to her under the sky, taught her the ropes of stargazing, sent her postcards, sung her sad songs, bought her beers and trinkets. Strangers had taken her into their homes, held her hand while crossing Stalin-era boulevards in bleak Eastern European cities, keeping her safe as they would a child. All the while she'd been a prideful young woman in her twenties, carried along by her sense of freedom and wanderlust, by her curiosity and cravings, wanting much more from the world than it had to offer.

As Claire Halde had grown older, she had grown out of the habit of falling in with groups of fellow travellers. Or at least that's what she tells herself as she stands in front of the oversized mirror in the bathroom adjoining her room, wiping the makeup off her eyes, bloodshot from the contact lenses scraping against her eyeballs—goddamned dry eye syndrome—the sun, and her flaking mascara.

In bed, she checks her Couchsurfing inbox, where she finds several replies to her couch request, mostly from men. Some just want to take her out for a drink, like Juan Carlos, or meet her for a short run. One offers to pick her up at the train station, another to put her up for a few nights at his seaside apartment in El Perelló, twenty-odd kilometres outside of Valencia. Manuel has attached pictures of the sunset and a table beautifully laid for breakfast on the patio—Italian coffee pot gleaming in the sun, orange juice in stemmed glasses, croissants and a glob of jam in a soup plate, white tablecloth—assuring her she'll have her own room and that he's very excited to meet her, that it'll be an honour for him to have her in his home. She accepts his invitation because he's the first to reply to her with so much enthusiasm and because, if the photos are to be believed, the horizon in El Perelló, with its blue sky and flat, waveless sea, promises to bring her some sense of peace.

KILOMETRE 21.1

... I can see the arch and the time clock signalling the half-marathon, one hour fifty-nine minutes, all good so far, I'm matching my breathing to my pace, with each step I take, I slowly exchange the air in my lungs with the air outside, no pain, just a perfect rhythm that evens out my movements, head straight and determined, focused on the action of running, lungs and heart in sync on my course across Valencia, I bear down on the port, the ships in their moorings stand out sharply against the sky, hulking metal monsters, I run toward *the most hostile point on the horizon*, the beauty of sea ports, departures, trips, they've always filled me with apprehension, *before you were born, Laure, your mother would take off at every chance she got, she was always like that, we couldn't get her to stay put...*

... my father had loved her, among other reasons, for her urge to travel to the farthest reaches of the planet, and when I read Flaubert, in French class in college, I'd automatically replaced the *him* in *Sentimental Education* with a *her*, hoping she'd be back—*she returned home*—memorizing that passage like a supplication that might one day bring my mother back to me, it's crazy, I still remember the quote word-for-word from my literature class:

She travelled a long time.

She experienced the melancholy associated with packet-boats, the chill feeling on waking up under tents, the dizzy effect of mountains and ruins, and the bitterness of broken sympathies.

She returned home.

... she did not return home, she still hasn't come home, all that remains are the photos from her trips, shoeboxes filled with pictures of unidentified volcanoes, glaciers, beaches and cities, eventually supplanted by a jumbled mess of misnamed computer files, my mother was a disaster, completely disorganized, never wrote anything on the backs of printed photos, all the snapshots of my childhood, birthdays and Christmases, first days of school, vacation memories and Halloween costumes—me as a ladybug, a witch, a princess in a poufy dress, buried up to my chin under a layer of sand, skipping among the ruins of Angkor, me with my first pigtails, covered in ice cream, on horseback next to a volcano, nose buried in a tropical drink, naked in the bathtub, asleep on a train, cheek pressed up against my blankie, smiling gap-toothed over a chocolate cake topped with strawberries—all stored in a single folder on her computer labelled *Pictures*, I find one of my mother with short hair, there aren't many pictures of her with long hair, there's one I like a lot, you're wearing a leather jacket, faded jeans, pretty red lipstick, you're my age, twenty-three, tangled brown locks blowing in the breeze, you're standing regally on the steps of the Trans-Siberian, at the station in Yekaterinburg, as though all the forests in Russia were your kingdom, a wide smile on your face, a happy young woman, cheeks rosy, eyes sparkling, a colourful wool shawl draped around your neck, I found it tucked away in a box, that floral-print shawl from Russia, moth-eaten and full of holes...

KILOMETRE 22

... we're back at the port of Valencia, I glance at the boats, the yachts, the flowerpots in the median, the palm trees, a playground surrounded by a fence that looks a lot like a candy necklace, now we're running through the misting station, like a lukewarm bath meant to bring down a fever, cooling off my neck and head, I'm braced from head to toe, my soul rinsed clean, bleached, a brief chill runs through my brain like I just chewed an ice cube, if only the same could be done with dark thoughts, wash them away...

KILOMETRE 23

... again with the dry mouth, I run my tongue over my lips, five minutes thirty-nine seconds, still okay, stay focused,

whenever her face pops into my mind, it's always got that same sad, clouded look on it, the expression from those last few days, sometimes my mother would stop mid-sentence during bedtime stories, and I could tell by the look in her eyes, the shadow passing over her face, that her thoughts were miles away from the fairy tales, one day at the grocery store, she opened up the ice cream freezer and just stood there, unmoving, staring at the cartons of lemon sorbet, forehead pressed up against the frosty door, Léon had tugged on her sleeve and asked: Are you okay, Mama? and she hadn't answered, we'd pushed past her to grab a tub of mint chocolate chip, then, without a word, she'd gone back to pushing the cart, and we'd trotted along behind her to the cash, my mother, already almost gone, hauling her grocery bags all the way home, serving us ice cream in deep bowls, then leaving us alone in front of the TV, *Mama will be home in a hour, I need to go for a run...*

KILOMETRE 24

... it feels like my body is turning to lead, everything wants to slow down, arms, legs aren't swinging as freely as they did before, I need to stay sharp, on the flyleaf of your running journal you'd written "Beware of the middle miles," a sentence from *The Competitive Runner's Handbook*, a guide you'd considered your Bible, a worn, dog-eared volume that I devoured hungrily, lingering on the passages you'd underlined and annotated—it's around the middle of the race, according to the author, that you tend to lose focus and fall off your pace—you'd taken a yellow highlighter to the pace charts, underlining the times you needed to pull off a 3:30 marathon, and converted the miles to kilometres, in your journal you'd also jotted down a list of mantras: "The worst is yet to come," "Just flow," the quote by Rilke again, "Just keep going. No feeling is final," and my favourite, "Relax your shoulders," I don't know if you actually repeated them to yourself while running, I think it's more like your head was filled with a bright light or a raging blizzard when you ran, or like a thick bank of fog rolled in and your brain became a fathomless ocean, a seabed untouched by doubt...

KILOMETRE 25

... I have this memory of my mother, a holiday in the islands, I must be nine or ten, I'm wearing an emerald-green bathing suit, my little brother is round and happy, collecting seashells and bits of broken crab shells, my mother takes me snorkelling, she adjusts my mask, it's tugging on my hair, I'm scared, but I really want to go, she shows me how to breathe, points to the looming black formations beneath the turquoise water, explains that they're coral reefs, we set out, the sun over our shoulders, I'm already a strong swimmer, my mother is holding my hand, I grasp her fingers tightly, I've never swum with so much water beneath me, we follow the schools of fish, we explore, my heart is pounding, my feet kicking, I swim in my mother's wake, I feel incredibly alive and so tiny compared to the deepness of the water, the marine life, I stay close to her, my hand folded into hers, then my mother gives my arm a tug and points to something, I don't see it at first, I look hard, there's so much to see, then it's right there in front of me, a giant sea turtle gliding along just a few metres away, I also remember seeing a stingray and feeling terrified as I watched it lurking in the sand, that moment alone with my mother is unlike any other during my childhood, beneath the surface of the water, in the oceanic silence, above the waving algae and the coral, transfixed by all the fish, enthralled by a second giant turtle drifting along the currents, we are suspended, tethered to one another, fingers intertwined, our breathing resonant and strange, majestic...

DAY 2 ITINERARY:
THE MAIN ATTRACTIONS

At breakfast, Claire sits across from an empty chair. She's surrounded by couples and families buttering their bread and sweetening their coffee. She notices a plate go by piled high with churros and chocolate-filled pastries, and it reminds her that she still hasn't sent postcards for the kids. Her hands are shaking; she pours her coffee, and her cup overflows, burning her fingers and leaving a huge, dark stain down the front of her white shirt. A tall German woman stares at her.

The night before, as she was walking around the pool, then near the changing room, to all appearances out for a casual stroll around the rooftop terrace or snapping photos leisurely in the hushed hotel corridors, it had occurred to her that, this time, she was the one who looked like a strange, sinister woman.

This morning, she climbs past the fifteenth floor, in the narrow staircase with the sign on the wall that reads *Acceso prohibido*, but in front of the heavy emergency exit door, her courage falters, she turns on her heel and goes back to her room, clenching her teeth so hard she chips the enamel. A tiny shard of tooth flakes off one of her incisors and rolls around in her mouth.

Late morning, Claire goes to the City of Arts and Sciences but doesn't buy a ticket for the Oceanogràfic, deterred by the lineup and the price of admission. Instead, she settles for a walk around the buildings.

In the pool near the Umbracle, children are having a grand time walking on water inside huge plastic bubbles—a contraption designed by NASA to help astronauts work on balance and resistance, which can be taken for a ten-minute test run in exchange for five euros. "Walking on water is similar to what astronauts feel when walking in zero gravity," a laminated sign reads.

She's reminded of that time when, on a beach in Thailand, to make Jean happy, she'd agreed to be harnessed to a giant kite and lifted into the sky at the end of a long rope attached to a speedboat. She hadn't really wanted to do it, but nor had she wanted to seem like the spoilsport who wasn't into thrill-seeking. Jean had gone first. She'd waved her arms back and forth at him, standing far below with the kids on the strip of wet sand. He'd come down after twenty minutes or so, eyes gleaming, grinning madly, insisting that she, too, be strapped in and given a turn to soar.

And so, she'd stood there with her arms raised out to her sides while a man adjusted the various straps and harnesses over her chest and between her legs. Her heart was beating faster than usual; she was nervous, a little pale. Once in the air, what had struck her most—more than the feeling of weightlessness or the magnificence of the view, which was indeed spectacular—was the absence of shouting and commotion. The wind and the flapping of the canvas were the only sounds. Silence was a measure of estrangement, of solitude. With one hand clenched over the carabiner, which would have been so easy to release, she'd let her eyes travel the length of the cable that was keeping her tethered to the packed beach like she no longer belonged to this world, far below, where her children waited for her next to their father.

THE CATHEDRAL

Claire takes a bus to the Plaza de la Virgen. She buys a ticket to climb to the top of the Miguelete, the cathedral tower. She can hear the people ahead of her on the steep stairs huffing and puffing. When she's forced to move over for tourists on their way down, she's unsettled by how close they come to her, like bodies pressed together in a crowded elevator. She detects the smell of sweat and perfume, the sighs and sways of bodies. Some people are less sure of themselves, clinging to the handrail, while others descend swiftly.

In the tower, the wind gets underneath her dress, exposing the tops of her thighs. She has to hold it down to keep her panties from showing. There's a security guard and a large bell that people are taking pictures under. The sun is already ruthless and it's not even noon yet. She takes in the panoramic view of the city. She searches in vain for the outline of the Valencia Palace. With the city spread out at her feet, she can't help thinking what it would be like to slip and fall from this height.

Whenever she's on a balcony, she sidles up to the edge and leans far out over the railing, ignoring the trembling in her legs and the feeling like the floor is caving in under her feet. When she runs over the Jacques Cartier Bridge, she can't stop herself from peering down at the green water swirling more than a hundred feet below. When she opens a window to air out her son's room, which faces the main street, when she washes the windows in her third-floor apartment, she's struck by the distinct impression she's putting her life in danger. Before Valencia, Claire Halde had never experienced vertigo.

BLOCKING THE VIEW

Claire travels Valencia by metro, bus, tram. She walks around in the crippling heat, runs along the dry riverbed, seeks out shade in the sun-baked streets. She wishes Valencia would open up for her like for an ordinary traveller. It's odd how she's forgotten the city and its monuments. But it's all coming back to her—the gargoyles on the Lonja de la Seda, the rose-tinted paving slabs in the Plaza de la Virgen, the bullfighting arena outside the train station. She writes almost nothing in her journal, barely takes any photos.

The ghost of the woman in Valencia looms large, but Claire delays her visit to the office of unclaimed bodies; she finds excuses, blames the time difference. The fog lingers. Instead of piecing together the woman in Valencia's story, she finds herself stumbling over her own narrative, which is blocking the view. She's become the main focus, everything here leading her right back to herself, her indifference, her fatigue. She thinks back to the Nicolas Bouvier quotation memorized from reading and rereading *The Way of the World* on all her travels; she'd inscribed it in red marker inside her very first backpack: "Travelling outgrows its motives. It soon proves sufficient in itself. You think you are making a trip, but soon it is making you—or unmaking you," and she wonders what happened to that longing for far-off places that had once consumed her, before.

KILOMETRE 26

... what I'd like, now that I've caught my breath, is to go in search of what was broken and lost here, I know full well that this race, this trivial effort of running 42.2 km in under four hours, won't save anything, won't bring my mother back, won't explain the inexplicable or console the inconsolable, yet I keep running, I run because, like my mother, I have a deep thirst, I don't want to be held back, I've come here looking for the light that my mother never found, or that she lost, I feel the need to speed up, the urge to raise my arms, flip off the world, show how fast and how well I can run, it's been a long time since I heard the concerned whispers—*those kids, those poor kids*—that no one dared utter in front of my brother and me, I'll show them that nothing can stop me, not heartbreak or loss, I slice through the air without slowing down, fuelled by fire and light, I won't falter, not me, I'll defy the odds, I'll fly in the face of tragedy, I'll throw it in their face—my triumph, my sub-four-hour marathon...

KILOMETRE 27

Elegant, you were born at night
Sewn by soft hands
Oh the softest hands
Born in solitude
Born of painted eyes
Painted eyes
That always looked to the sky
Oh those eyes
Oh those eyes
They saw forever

... you always liked this song, were always playing it at home and in the car, I like it, too, I don't know what there is about it, something funny about the rhythm that makes me feel light and bouncy, like I'm taking flight with each step, I find my fire again, I speed up, that kilometre flew by...

Oh those eyes
They saw forever

KILOMETRE 28

... as I'm running, I'm thinking about how you also ran in Valencia, not a marathon, but dozens of kilometres nonetheless, the day after that incident on the roof, you'd written in your journal: "I have to keep moving," and when you eventually returned to the city, I have no idea where your steps took you, you were training for the Chicago marathon at the time, which you never ended up running, I wonder if you're running still...

... I'm worried about my brother, you know, with all his manias and compulsions, he's the one who suffered most when you left because he didn't have the words, he also didn't have the anger he would have needed to release the tension, he never accepted your disappearance, he's still waiting for you, patiently, like the little boy who used to call out for a bedtime story from beneath the covers, do you remember that story about a civilization of tiny people who lived in a tree, the book we got for Christmas that I didn't want to read because I thought it was boring, Toby who ends up on the run searching for his parents, that story that you read to him, and only him, one chapter at a time? I can picture you snuggled up next to my little brother, folded awkwardly on his narrow bed, your voice soft and gentle when really you must have already been falling apart, it was me who read him the second book after you left, Dad didn't have the heart for it, after all the adventures and all the misfortune, everyone was reunited and lived happily ever after...

KILOMETRE 29

... Plaza del Ayuntamiento, I was near here yesterday, over there, I think, I drank an ice-cold *horchata*, this two-hundred-year-old square with the pretty ceramic, I have a picture of me as a kid in this same spot, I'm licking my fingers, the tip of my nose is dusted with powdered sugar, I'm sitting next to my mother who's got one elbow propped on the white marble, head resting in her palm, staring off into space, somewhere off camera, her face creased with exhaustion, and that same shuttered expression that always made her look so mysterious—a patrician arrangement of features, an aristocratic countenance that always, in all circumstances, gave off the vibe of a woman impossible to read, on her wrist she's wearing a twisted bracelet, which I claimed and now wear for special occasions...

KILOMETRE 30

... I spot the bullfighting arena on my left and the massive train station, Estació del Nord, straight ahead, headed in the opposite direction, the fast runners are already on their last few kilometres, just look at their form, like wild animals, as for me, I've still got a long way to go, a church and a few shops, finally some shade, a slanted building in the distance, the MuVIM gardens in the intersection, I have a better idea of where I am now, all those faces in the crowd, there's no way she's in there, how is it that after all these years I'm still hoping she'll appear, I was twelve the last time she saw me, flat as a board, nothing but tiny buds, no hips, hair down to my bum, I was chubby and carefree, always smiling, people said I looked like my father, that I had his eyes but my grandmother's forehead, now, people who knew my mother sometimes tell me, voices cracking with emotion: It's crazy how much you remind me of her, you've got the same smile, there's an aid station coming up, gels and fruit, don't want to miss it...

THREATS AND EMERGENCIES

Claire Halde walks toward the office of unclaimed bodies, large mauve purse hooked over her elbow, cutting
off the circulation in the same spot where you might
cradle the head of a sleeping baby.

Since arriving, when walking around Valencia, Claire
has made a point of noticing the people she passes on
the street, the expressions on their faces, the way they
walk, their hugs and kisses, and their tone of voice as
they exchange greetings or information, or even mun-
dane questions about the direction of a bus, the location
of a store, the time. People don't ask for the time nearly
as much as they used to.

It seems to her that the people here are warmer. That
much is obvious from the familiar and intimate ways
they interact with each other: a hand on a shoulder, an
arm around a waist, a genuine compliment between
neighbours, a face cupped gently between two hands,
a certain way of kissing, greeting each other, folding
an acquaintance into a warm embrace on the sidewalk.

She also thinks they talk to each other with more affection, more spontaneity. She's conscious of her North American coldness, her uptight mannerisms, her lukewarm kisses, given out only when she has no other choice, in her own city or anywhere else in the world: head tilted to the right, cheek angled to the left, by way of hello, goodbye, nice to meet you.

She watches the people seated around a table at a café near the courthouse, the way they drink, eat, smoke, look at each other, the hand gestures and facial expressions that accompany their conversations, silences, peals of laughter. More than ever, she feels like an aloof foreigner as she takes the concrete steps two at a time in front of the Institute of Legal Medicine, on Carrer de Ricardo Muñoz Suay. The purse sways back and forth, a mauve metronome that skips a beat when Claire stops short on the landing. She takes a second to close her eyes and release her jaw, clenched too tight as always. She lets out a sigh, pushes open the door.

UNFORESEEN EVENTS

Claire had played out the scene dozens of times in her mind, running the sentences over in her head, getting the Spanish exactly right. She'd read up on the subject. Unclaimed bodies were stored for a time in the morgue at Ciudad Hospitalaria Dr. Enrique Tejera, in cold rooms kept at three degrees Celsius, behind sealed doors opened only by court order. Next of kin had forty-eight hours to come forward and identify the deceased. Failing that, the cadavers were sent to the Faculty of Medicine's anatomy department, for the students to dissect. Afterwards, the remains were buried in the public cemetery.

For each unclaimed body, fingerprints were taken, the items found with the deceased were photographed and a sample was collected for possible DNA testing.

Claire's voice quavers as she pronounces the date of August 9, 2009, to the clerk behind the counter. A woman, found dead on Avinguda de las Cortes Valencianas, she specifies, clutching the oversized purse against her hip. The employee shakes her head categorically.

"We have no women on file for that date."

Claire asks her to check the records for the few days before, the few days after. There's no match for the woman in Valencia.

"You can always try your luck at the registry office," the clerk smiles. "You'll have to fill out the appropriate forms, of course."

"Of course," Claire murmurs.

She exits the office in reverse, shoving the door open with her back, and bounds down the stairs even faster than she ran up them. She crosses the paved square in front of the courthouse at a clip, heels clicking on the asphalt like horseshoes or heavy wooden clogs. She speeds up in front of the police station, crosses Avinguda del Profesor López Piñero without a second thought for the light that's just turned red. Purse still dangling from her arm, she runs, rushing onto Avinguda Autopista del Saler, bearing down on the Umbracle and its palm trees. She hurries into the covered garden without slowing, hurdling rosemary and lavender bushes, trampling fragrant thyme plants, slaloming around bougainvillea and dwarf orange trees. She elbows her way through tourists clustered next to the ponds, bolts across the Río like a spooked horse, to emerge crazed on Passeig de l'Albereda, which she crosses panting for breath. She forges ahead randomly, turning left two streets later, and sprints ahead in a straight line until she's gasping for air, barely making it to the next intersection, where she catches a glimpse of her reflection, scarlet and dishevelled, in the window of a starkly decorated hair salon on the corner of Carrer de Trafalgar. Then, without slowing her pace, lungs screaming for air, she barges through the door as one would send out a pawn: rashly, hoping for the best.

"A cut and colour. Do you have room? Like, right now?"

KILOMETRE 31

... from here on in, it's all an unknown quantity, I've never run more than thirty kilometres before, it's okay, I know things could go sideways, starting now, it's a head game, too...

... my mother, after Valencia, was obsessed with death, she hid her distress well, her friends all told me stories about what an outgoing and funny and smiling person my mother was, about how tender and loving and happy she was with us, everyone painted the same picture of her, stressing her remarkable intelligence, her piercing gaze, but also the gentle way she had about her,

my mother, head of the class, spelling bee champion and mathletics winner, loyal and dedicated friend, completely genuine, always thinking of others, especially her children, putting our happiness ahead of her own, according to my grandmother, deeply sensitive, even her skin reacted to the slightest aggression, the cold, the heat, the water, she suffered from a condition that I inherited to a milder degree, dermographism, an exaggerated form of hives, even the slightest graze with a fingernail was enough to cause red wheals to appear on her skin, and after she stepped out of the shower, each and every rub and wipe of the towel was apparent from the scarlet lines left behind on her body,

my mother, queen of repartee, who had a way of laughing at herself and of always seeing the beauty in things, who insisted on always looking for the silver lining, with a casualness that we assumed made her impervious to drama, sometimes she'd write "I love you" on her forearm for us, and her skin would immediately come up in red, letter-shaped welts that eventually faded to white,

before Valencia, my mother had been a perfect mother, an all-around perfect woman who nevertheless abandoned us in August 2015, *we don't understand it, Laure, there's got to be an explanation, it's not like your mother to just disappear,* and yet, the explanation never came, and my mother, my famous perfect mother, stunning, unreal, never came back either...

KILOMETRE 32

... it's been ages since I looked for you like I used to when I was a kid, buoyed by the belief that you might suddenly appear at any moment, that I'd open my eyes one night and find you standing right in front of me in my room, and the darkness would fade away, there were times I felt furious, I hated you for it, but now I know I'd welcome you with open arms if you came back, I'd forgive you for deserting us,

if only we could know, if only the answers to all life's mysteries and affronts were written somewhere, if only we could understand what hurts people, what drives others to do this or that, you've become a woman I've stopped hoping will appear at any minute around every corner, every time the doorbell buzzes or the phone rings, the hope is still there, even though it's fading, I go on waiting, for you to appear,

but how could I ever give up hope of seeing you again unless a police officer actually knocked on the door to tell us there's been a development, they've found your body, they've picked up your trail? I've often told myself that maybe you're adrift somewhere, suffering from amnesia, that you didn't actually abandon us, all of us, your son and daughter, your friends, your mother, your sister, your cat, maybe you've simply just forgotten everything, down to your name and address, maybe you don't know you're supposed to be looking for us, that's why you haven't come back to us, I refuse to believe that you're dead, no, you didn't want to die, just disappear, run away, and now it's me running through Valencia, like I'm heading out to meet you...

Run, my love, run! You can do it!

... on my way past, I give the thirty-two kilometre marker, that wall that everyone goes on about, a discreet flying finger, fist pressed tightly against my thigh, middle finger standing tall—take that, you won't get the best of me—here's where the marathon gets serious, the last ten kilometres can break a runner...

KILOMETRE 33

... just keep going, my body's a battlefield, why? why am I doing this to myself? the repetitive motion, the pain, the chafing skin and searing muscles, the spaghetti arms, the cement in my legs, the toes on fire in my running shoes, I'm not going to make it, I'm not even sure if it's my mind or my body that's ready to give up, the seam on this tank top is killing me, a nail file rubbing against my collarbone, the skin under my armpit is chafed red and raw, I lean into the gusting wind, *wild is the wind*, I put one foot down, then the other, I raise one arm, then the other, I breathe in, I breathe out, legs like lead,

I try to ignore the stiffness, not think about it, I keep going, keeping running, five minutes fifty seconds per kilometre, I've slowed down, no matter how hard I try, I'm losing steam, but what was I thinking? a marathon in under four hours, but why? pulse pounding in my temples, sickly sweet taste in my mouth, hips screaming in pain, neck stiff and aching, I block out the pain, I ignore my brain begging me to slow down, I refuse to give in to everything that's trying to hold me back, *we don't go there*, my mother used to say...

Relax your shoulders.
Relax your shoulders.
Relax your shoulders.

KILOMETRE 34

... I'm tired, so tired, I don't want to stop and I don't want to slow down, the effort is more than I've got in me, I need to keep going, my mind is made up, failure is not an option, weakness is not permitted, no body of mine is going to give up and give out, c'mon, eight kilometres to go, the soles of my feet are burning, my heel is throbbing, my toes are chafing, stay focused, don't slow down, I pump my arms, I lift one foot, I land, I push off, straining and leaning my whole body forward, trying to tap into my inner ferocity, I'm only at kilometre 34, I'm hanging on for dear life, everything is shutting down, I keep running...

KILOMETRE 35

... I can't do it, I want it to stop, everything is falling apart, I'm a big ball of pain, my whole body hurts, I'm thirsty but I'm not thirsty, I feel like I might throw up any second now, I just want it to stop, the movement, the absurdly repetitive movement, the fatigue, the hard ground, the stiffness in my calves and quads, it's radiating, shooting straight to my nerves, why is everything so heavy? I look to my left, there's a man worse off than I am, he's not even running anymore, he's staggering, he's about to collapse, go on, buck up, I toss him a smile like a life preserver that he fails to catch, each stride is like a jackhammer to my body, each slap of my soles against the pavement like I'm slowly drowning, sinking in quicksand, I need to keep going, keep going, keep going, moving forward, seven kilometres to go, seven times six, forty-odd minutes, I can't even count anymore, oh well, just keep running...

HAIR CARE

I want a new hairstyle, Claire explains to the hair-dresser. No, there was no breakup. No, not Venetian blonde. Something else. I don't know the Spanish word for that shade of blonde. Something cooler, classic, but a little retro. You know, like Eva Marie Saint in *North by Northwest*? Or Tippi Hedren in *The Birds*? No? What about Kim Novak in *Vertigo*? Wait. Naomi Watts in *Mulholland Drive*? But really short, a pixie cut à la Jean Seberg. Hmm, not recommended on a woman with a strong jaw? Okay. A layered bob, yes, I see, alright, let's go with a layered bob, in a frosted blonde.

VALENCIA PALACE HOTEL

Late in the day, Claire returns to her room, even though she doesn't feel like it. It's evening, in a bed nothing like her own, permeated with the strangeness of her return to Valencia. Her brain is addled by fatigue. Her skin is stinging—she's skimping on the sunscreen—and her muscles are twitching from all the walking. She stares at the walls and ceiling, lets herself sink into the dense hotel silence. She eyes the big mauve purse that she'd set down between the TV and the single-serve coffeemaker, not yet ready to abandon it in a deserted corner of the hotel or a public place.

Lying there in the dull room, taking in the ordinary ugliness of the furniture, she's struck by a sense of loneliness. It occurs to her how these temporary spaces all end up looking the same, a revolving door of rooms for interchangeable travellers. Claire wonders who slept in this bed before her, how many bodies have been stretched out on this mattress, and what their nights were like. She thinks about the guests who have preceded her and ponders whether any trace still lingers in the air, in this room, of their dreams, their insomnia, their love affairs, their solitude, their loneliness, their bouts of misery or terror.

She wonders if it was a smart move to accept the invitation from that Manuel guy, whom she knows absolutely nothing about, and who's messaged her to confirm their meeting spot for the next day, adding: "I'll bring some poems by García Lorca, we can read them together." Claire sometimes thinks she's become blasé, that time has turned her bourgeois. How else to explain how she ended up on the rooftop terrace of a four-star hotel next to a congress centre, in a half-dead neighbourhood, and looked on with indifference as a stranger, wrist dripping with blood, hurled herself into the void on a summer afternoon? When Manuel inevitably asks her, in Benicalap Park, if she's been many places, if she often travels alone like this, she won't have the slightest desire to get into details.

THE LOCALS

They've agreed to meet two blocks away from the hotel. She's waiting for him, sitting on a concrete block, her rolling suitcase squeezed between her thighs, balanced precariously. Twice, the heavy case tips over on the sidewalk with a thud. The bottles of perfume she bought in Barcelona remain intact. She scrutinizes all the single men walking by. None of them smile at her, none seem like they're looking for her. There's a dour-looking man seated on a restaurant patio, chewing angrily on a mostly rare steak. With his black hair and bushy eyebrows, he bears a vague resemblance to the Manuel she's waiting for, although she's only seen one blurry photo of him, and he was wearing sunglasses. She's wavering back and forth about approaching him, hoping it's not him. There's something disagreeable—impatience and sternness— radiating off his body and from his harsh expression.

Eventually, an old Mercedes pulls up. The driver looks in her direction, worried, then reassured. It's definitely her, that woman with the suitcase, legs crossed nonchalantly.

He parks quickly, in a few deft moves, then gets out of his car, slamming the door behind him. Looking every inch the Javier Bardem, she thinks, watching him cross the street. He's wearing black jeans despite the heat, Ray-Bans, and has a weird haircut with long strands growing down the back of his neck like pointy rattails, which he musses with one hand as he strides toward her.

"My English is not too good. I'm Anna from Russia. *Hablo español*," she offers by way of an introduction.

He smells like cigarette smoke. Before long, he'll confess that he's had nothing to eat since that morning, since leaving Madrid, apart from black coffee to stay alert at the wheel, too nervous at the thought of meeting her.

Claire tells herself it's been a long time since she's made a man too flustered to eat. She studies his face. His expression belies a certain gentleness, despite his bad boy appearance. She instantly feels like she can trust him. It's hard to explain, you can't always put your finger on it—the tone of voice or the tentative gaze—and suddenly you're hoisting your suitcase into the trunk of a stranger's car. They walk side by side toward Benicalap Park, and she points out the strange outline of the Valencia Palace Hotel. In five minutes flat, she's spilled the story that she could never even bring herself to tell her mother, her sister, her shrink.

WORTH THE DETOUR:
THE VALENCIA INSTITUTE OF MODERN ART

As they'd agreed in their messages on couchsurfing.com, Manuel and Claire would spend the day together before heading to the apartment in El Perelló. Astonishingly, it turns out she knows Valencia better than he does. He'd spent every summer since he was a little boy in the apartment twenty minutes outside of the city without ever really exploring it or learning his way around. He had only vague memories of his visits and doesn't know the names of the cathedrals or any good places to eat. She never lets on otherwise, but Claire secretly views this lack of curiosity, this travel apathy, with contempt. She gives him an indulgent smile and pulls out her city map, smoothing out the wrinkles with her fingers.

"I'm from Madrid," he apologizes. "A *Madrileño*, born and bred."

So, she guides the *Madrileño* through the winding streets of Ciutat Vella, introduces him to the murals painted by an Argentinian artist, navigates them to the Valencia Institute of Modern Art, tells him about the Nan Goldin photos that made such an impression on her during her last visit that she went to see them twice more in New York. To see them strolling together from painting to painting, whispering about their likes and dislikes, you'd never guess that they'd only just met at noon that same day. They stand next to each other, shoulders touching lightly, transfixed by that famous scene from *Battleship Potemkin*—the black-veiled woman, her face contorted with pain, and the runaway baby carriage with the oversized wheels barrelling down the Odessa steps for what feels like an eternity—projected in an endless loop on a wall of the exhibition hall.

The hours pass in silence. They wander from the Dadaists to the Surrealists, then to a collection of posters dating from the Franco dictatorship, where they don't linger. This wouldn't really interest you, he asserts. She doesn't force the issue.

NOT TO BE MISSED:
MERCADO DE COLÓN

After touring the museum, they walk over to the Mercado de Colón to meet up with Juan Carlos, a man with a strong jaw, bright gaze, hair as short as his fingernails. While mostly a homebody, he gets a kick out of meeting other travellers. He's the unofficial doyen of couchsurfing in Valencia, always proud to show off his city, host strangers, cook a paella for his new friends.

The trio orders cocktails. The conversation flows easily. Juan Carlos asks Claire what brings her to Valencia. I'm here to write a screenplay, she lies with surprising ease. They look at her with interest, eager for more details. For effect, she adopts a serious tone and launches into detail: The woman is blonde and injured, the sky is hazy, the scene a stifling rooftop terrace of a hotel, there's an atmosphere of unease, worry, mystery running through the film, we don't know who the woman is, and we never find out, she ends up jumping off the roof, we don't know why. Manuel and Juan Carlos put forward hypotheses: Maybe she was this, or that, you need to invent a life for her.

"I've never met a filmmaker before," Manuel marvels. Claire smiles modestly, looks down at her sandals, answers that, at the moment, there's no actual movie, only a screenplay.

"Obviously, it would make a great movie," Juan Carlos adds. "It's got everything: mood, drama, mystery, setting, you're on to something here."

Claire smiles again, amazed at how well she's keeping up the lie. Juan Carlos starts talking about a neighbour, a Valencian who jumped out a window the month before and landed in front of the kiosk belonging to the flower seller, who had to be taken to hospital for shock. Everywhere, at all hours of the day, people are killing themselves, taking their lives.

Claire doesn't elaborate on her plans or her personal life: "The children are staying with their father for ten days. We haven't lived together for four years." Juan Carlos corrects her when she stumbles over her Spanish verb tenses or flubs a subjunctive. She studies him closely, blown away by his confidence, his calm expression, the large hands of a fluid mechanical engineer. She's almost sorry he didn't offer to put her up and wonders if she wouldn't have been better off staying with this utterly decent, impeccably groomed man, accustomed to taking things in hand, to solving problems, to studying the behaviour of bubbles and whirlpools.

"They may seem straightforward, but bubbles are often unpredictable, in both the shapes they take and their trajectories," he explains to them. "A little like people, like chance meetings, Anna," he adds, smiling at Claire. Even though they're both forty, next to Juan Carlos, Manuel looks like a ragamuffin or an overgrown teenager. And it's too late now for a change of plans.

IN THE CAR

It's late when they finally get back to the car after parting ways with Juan Carlos, at the end of a leisurely meal of Andalusian tapas. Claire and Manuel had to run to catch the last metro, which lets them off near the Valencia Palace.

Manuel is nervous. His phone is dead, and he doesn't know his way out of Valencia. His phone charger is frayed, so he asks Claire to hold it at a certain angle to keep the wires together. She can't get the hang of it. The GPS keeps flickering on and off.

"Left," she says, consulting the screen.

"Here?"

"No, the next one."

Too late. He turns left down the first street.

"The next one! You were supposed to take the next one."

On her right, she notices a sign, a circle with a diagonal line through it. Everything is happening very quickly. The headlights glint off a set of rails on the ground.

"The tramway! We're on the tram tracks!"

Above their heads, a set of parallel lines hangs slackly. Manuel squirms in his seat, a mortified look on his face. He runs a hand through his hair, steps on the gas. *We're going to die, we're going to die right here, just steps away from the Valencia Palace.* They hit a curb. The noise is ominous: once, twice, the sound of grinding metal. Manuel jerks the wheel to the right, and the car finally frees itself from the tracks.

He pulls over a little further along, on a deserted, poorly lit street. He scrubs his hands over his face, presses his fingers against his eyelids. Claire isn't sure what to do with herself. She stays frozen in her seat, strapped in by the safety belt, head turned toward the window and the blackness of the night beyond.

As though addressing her own reflection in the glass—that blonde figure she can't quite reconcile herself with—she conducts a silent interview, summing up the situation dispassionately: It's after midnight, you're in a car with a man you don't know, on the outskirts of a dispiriting city, and you could have just died together, mown down by a tram. Maybe, deep down, you don't really care all that much if you live or die, she observes even more starkly.

Manuel grabs his phone and calls his mother on speaker. The confused voice of an elderly lady comes over the line:

"You woke me up. Where are you?"

"I'm in Valencia with a friend. She's from Russia."

Claire continues to stare out the window, into the blackness. She imagines the old woman in her Madrid apartment, in her nightgown, head covered with thick, dull hair, skin speckled with age spots.

"I'm worried about you."

"Everything's fine, Mama, I love you," he answers, his voice breaking.

It makes Claire Halde uncomfortable to see this man, whose self-assurance had been so impressive seven hours earlier, now acting like a little boy about to dissolve into a puddle of hiccupping sobs, calling his elderly mother for comfort instead of turning to her.

He finally hangs up. He apologizes to Claire, tells her he feels terrible, that he understands if she doesn't trust him anymore. She replies matter-of-factly, "It's fine, but what about your car? We still need to get where we're going, get out of this goddamned city."

She wants to go to sleep, huddle up in bed, finally be alone for a minute so she can process this bizarre day. Manuel steps out of the car, gets down on all fours on one side, then the other. He sighs profusely, but his voice is steady. Everything seems fine. He doesn't see any leaks. He slides back in behind the wheel, lets out another long sigh, wipes his forehead with his arm, then turns the key.

They ease back onto the road, finally finding the entrance to the highway on the other side of the Valencia Palace. I never want to see this place again, Claire Halde thinks as the car picks up speed.

GETTING ORIENTED

The car flies down the highway, and Manuel is still on edge. They've lost the GPS again, after giving up on trying to hold the cord just so. Without a signal, they're navigating mostly on instinct. The silence in the car is oppressive. Claire hazards a question: Do you know where you're going? Does anything look familiar? He mumbles something not at all reassuring. She keeps her eyes pointed forward.

The alcohol is mostly out of her system by now, and this whole business suddenly seems like a bad idea. Her jaw clenches. The Mercedes enters a roundabout. Manuel hesitates over which way to go—he's obviously never been here before—and opts for an extra spin around the traffic circle. Claire feels dizzy, and the constant turning is making her queasy. She feels like their circular trajectory might never stop, like the car might keep going indefinitely, around and around this paved circle without ever finding a way out. She snaps out of it and reads the road signs out to Manuel, who finally takes one of the exits marked on the bright blue panel.

Darkness surrounds them, making it difficult to get their bearings. There's not a building or a tree in sight, let alone any sign of human life; the glow of a distant streetlamp grows dimmer. Manuel accelerates, revving the engine. They pass a stretch of dull, colourless fields, like a steppe that's suddenly sprung up on the outskirts of Valencia, in the precise spot where the guidebooks say they should see a freshwater lake surrounded by rice fields, orange trees, grapevines, almond plantations. They roll on in silence, unsettled by the gritty landscape, until the road ends abruptly. A row of concrete blocks bars their way. They're surrounded by a sea of dry, straggly grass, and everywhere, dust. The night is filled with the sound of crickets chirping. A huge billboard advertises a water park some ten kilometres away: a bikini-clad mother, with tanned skin and impossibly white teeth, arms wrapped around her children, who are wriggling with excitement, their bottoms squeezed into oversized inner tubes. *Okay, so this is where it happens, in this deserted field, this is where five men are going to jump out, rape you, and toss your body in the last clump of bushes around that hasn't yet crumbled to dust, in the middle of nowhere, and burn your passport.* The thought grows inside her, solidifies: *You fell for it, you silly bitch, that's what happens when you think you're invincible. They'll say: She asked for it, seriously, it wasn't going to end well.* A deep pit opens up inside her, like the night has just swallowed up a piece of her stomach.

Without a word, Manuel throws the car in reverse, drives back to the roundabout, takes a different exit this time. As they skirt Valencia, still not sure where they're going, the skies open up. The rain starts to come down harder, the wipers punctuating the thick silence hanging between them with a steady swish-thunk. They're beginning to second-guess the entire plan. At this point in the night, a distance, a feeling of mistrust even, creeps into the vehicle, between their two surly selves. Manuel asks: Does it bother you if I smoke in the car? She shakes her head no, go ahead and smoke. They roll down their windows a crack, enough to let in a stream of cold air, a few drops of drizzle. Claire lights up her own cigarette, coughs a little. A tendril of smoke drifts up to her face, burning her eyes and throat. She would have preferred something other than a Marlboro to calm her down—a scotch, maybe, or a sleeping pill.

Outside, everything is magnified and amplified—the movement of the windshield wipers, the rain drumming against the window, the howling of the wind, the carbon-paper blackness of the night—while, inside her head, her thoughts are swirling in slow motion, as though she were sliding into a drug-induced sleep, her pulse growing weaker. Her lungs feel like they're filling with white glue. Claire closes her eyes, tells herself everything will be fine, they can't be that lost. *Keep going, no feeling is final.*

EL PERELLÓ

We're here, he says. The headlights light up a street covered in water, deserted at this time of night. They look for a parking space, get themselves turned around for a brief minute. He points triumphantly to the building where they'll spend the next three nights, but they keep driving, finally coming to a stop some two hundred metres from the front door.

They grab their luggage and make a break for it, getting their feet soaking wet. They end up with hair plastered to their foreheads, ankles and calves splattered with warm, dirty water. Finally, Manuel pushes open a door, lets Claire walk through ahead of him. It's a building right on the sea, with a spacious lobby covered floor to ceiling in tiles, complete with tiled mural. There's a potted plant in one corner and a lone lightbulb hanging from the ceiling, around which insects buzz incessantly until they drop to the ground from exhaustion.

They step into a slow, tiny elevator, so cramped their hips are touching, the suitcase taking up one-third of the available space. On the sixth floor, he lets her out first, motioning her to go right with a jerk of his head. He brings a set of keys up to his face, explains how the lock works. The keys jangle, and the door swings open into a dark apartment. A dank smell permeates the air, laced with bleach and musty towel. A whiff of salt air, too, embedded in the wallpaper.

He flicks a switch, and the yellow glow from a bare lightbulb illuminates the outmoded decor of an apartment frozen in time.

So, this is my family's summer place, he says. One by one, he gives her a tour of the rooms where he and his brothers spent their vacations as children. She chooses one and sets her suitcase down at the foot of a colonial-style bed draped in a dusty rose duvet. There's only one opening in the wall for ventilation, a window as narrow as an arrow slit, which looks onto an empty, paved square shared with the neighbouring apartments. Claire sticks her head out. She looks up—she can't make out the sky, it's dark and murky, stifling—then looks down: The sight of the concrete six floors below makes her dizzy. In a flash, she pictures her body pitching forward over the edge, like a carp leaping through the air, then disappearing. She takes a step back, her face betraying nothing of her disturbing thoughts.

She follows Manuel into the kitchen. A fluorescent light buzzes on the ceiling, the empty refrigerator hums. The counter is bare save for a jug of water and a percolator; not much to see. Manuel switches off the light and asks Claire not to turn it on if she comes into the kitchen at night: It bothers the old lady next door, who's a light sleeper, and she'll find any excuse to complain. There's a balcony off the living room that overlooks the beach, the sea and a starless sky that's barely discernible, engulfed in a summer rain.

The sun first thing in the morning is already blinding. Claire moves silently down the long hallway leading to the balcony. The French door was left open all night. The air is fresh; the sea, a flat, dark line. The metal chairs gleam on the patio, the concrete looks even whiter in the bright sunlight. The rain from the night before has evaporated without a trace.

Claire looks left, then right. The beach is completely empty—no vegetation, no greenery, no birds—and bordered by a cement wall; a beach so colourless it might have been dipped in peroxide. The town at dawn is so completely silent, you'd think it had been drained of all life, razed by the whiteness emanating from the sky, by a blinding flash, a dagger of light.

She approaches the railing, grabs onto it. Her fingers curl tightly around the metal, turning pink like delicate parrot's feet on an incandescent perch. She needs something to lean on for support, to be able to peer six floors down. Ochre- and cream-coloured tiles form a mosaic on the ground. She takes a step back. There's that feeling again: calves giving out on her, muscles dissolving into a puddle, ankles wobbling—the feeling like she might lose her footing at any minute. Claire sits down, the chair searing hot under her thighs. In an attempt to banish the mental image of her body shattering on the ground six floors below, she stares off into the distance, tracking the odd holiday-goer already up and about in the sleepy resort town. Life at dawn moves in slow motion, to the muffled sound of the waves, the background music to the luxurious laziness of summer vacation. She sees a few people, elderly for the most part, out for their constitutional on the beach, walking their dogs, going for a morning jog, sweeping sand off the floor tiles.

Manuel is still sleeping. Claire slips on a pair of shorts, a tank top and running shoes, and straightens her hair. The sweat is already beading on the back of her neck. It's going to be a hot one. On the table in the entryway, she finds the set of keys, which she stuffs into her shorts pocket along with a twenty-euro bill. She leaves the apartment, closing the door softly behind her. She doesn't leave a note on the table; let Manuel worry if he wakes up.

She runs in a straight line, parallel to the sea. It's quiet here; the people she passes look hale and hardy, tanned and relaxed, like nothing in this vacation village could faze them. Bit by bit, the stiffness drains from her body, and she lets herself be lulled by the ocean air, the dazzling sun. Her jaw softens.

What an amazing machine the heart is, Claire has thought ever since she first started running a few years ago, coming to the sport at the age of thirty-three, marvelling at the sheer power of the organ, which she'd never really overtaxed up to that point, not even as a small child or a teenager.

With as much vehemence as most of her classmates, the young Claire Halde had detested running laps around the oval track behind the high school. She'd despised the awkward business of hurdles and the dreaded prospect of her shinbones cracking against the sharp gates with each running leap of her clumsy, gawky teenage girl's body, breasts bouncing in her Fruit of the Loom cotton granny bra. She'd held an equal loathing for gymnastics—her balance beam jumps performed with no grace whatsoever—lap swimming, and the brazen nudity and immature antics of the locker room. She'd cursed her legs, for having to be waxed before gym class, and that goddamned bush of a bikini area, for having to be shaved before each pool session. For Claire, physical activity had always been a series of humiliations she'd had to endure, all the while envying the lithe, slender, perfectly hairless bodies of the pretty girls. The girls with the flat, toned stomachs and the bouncy ponytails who knew how to throw a javelin without bashing themselves in the back of the head, who shrieked with excitement when the gym teacher announced they'd be playing a team sport, who year after year made the cut for the regional track-and-field meets. She vividly remembers the forearms left red and smarting from volleyball serves, the missed passes, the bad throws, bad catches, bad bounces and bad kicks. Then there was the rope climb; she'd never forget that coarse rope, dangling there from the wall bars, and the sheer agony of having to hoist herself up its seemingly endless length, knot by knot, like an inmate scaling a prison wall. No, Claire Halde had never liked sports, and as for her heart, she'd mostly gone easy on it before taking up marathon running. She'd never given much thought to her heartbeat before, but now she craved that invigorating feeling, that energy burn of a hard workout, that furious acceleration of arms and legs as she ran, propelled forward, bounding along as though fleeing a tiger or a killer.

Before returning to Manuel, she stops at the supermarket to pick up coffee and oranges, pastries and jam, milk, a stick of butter, eggs. She waits a long time for the elevator, her skin damp, bag of provisions under her arm, smiling at the thought of a man waking up happy to eat breakfast with her.

KILOMETRE 36

... I think about you, Mama, I cling to the thought, I picture you running in your red dress, perpetually on the
run in your red dress, according to the investigation Dad
ordered into your disappearance, you spent three nights
at the Valencia Palace Hotel, then nothing, an ATM
withdrawal at the Madrid train station and two more in
Seville to empty your bank accounts, but your name was
nowhere to be found at any of the hotels in the Spanish
capital or in Andalusia, in the CCTV pictures, we can
see you, blonde, wearing that strapless red dress that
no one recognized, not Dad or your friends—*she always
wore classic grey*—you're alone, you look good, a woman
on the run maybe, but not running scared...

KILOMETRE 37

It doesn't hurt me
Do you want to feel how it feels?

... I turn up the volume...
And if I only could
I'd make a deal with God
And I'd get him to swap our places
Be running up that road
Be running up that hill
Be running up that building
If I only could, oh

THE PRETTIEST BEACHES IN VALENCIA

To make Manuel happy, Claire spreads a towel out on the sand after breakfast, peels off her dress, kicks off her sandals. She sits facing the sea, legs stretched out, back loosely curved, forearms supporting her weight, elbows at right angles, stomach muscles flexed. Her body can be summed up in one word: *tense*. She's not one of those girls who enjoys lazing around on the beach, working on her tan, and it shows. She soaks in the lines of the horizon, the sound and motion of the waves, the sea foam.

Manuel is a sun worshipper. His chest is flawlessly tanned, in stark contrast to his white Adidas swim trunks with black stipes down the side seams. Swim trunks that look very good on him. Very, very good, Claire notes. It takes a certain amount of confidence and the perfect tan to pull off a bathing suit that white, Claire thinks, adjusting her rather modest navy bikini.

Claire concentrates hard, focusing all her attention on the seascape in an effort to cover up her boredom. It's the middle of the summer, and she's barely seen more than a few waves. The heat is sweltering, the sand is scorching, the air is stifling. People flock to this place precisely for the heat: to bronze their bodies, to bathe in the sea while the weather's still fine, because the children love to build sand castles.

Manuel splashes around in the water; she watches him from a distance behind her shades. There's something irritating about his way of barrelling into the waves like a raging animal. He carries himself with all the assurance of a hot guy, only less hot.

When he returns, Claire's nose is buried in a book and she pretends to be engrossed in her reading. Rather than grab a towel to dry off with or stretch out on the beach to let terrycloth and sunshine do their work, he starts moving around vigorously, performing a series of rapid-fire pushups in the sand. Droplets of water fly off his body, tiny liquid sparks that gleam in the light. Claire stares at her book, distracted by his athletic prowess, but not wanting to let on.

⌒

Around 11 a.m., Claire takes out her tube of sunscreen and slathers it all over her arms and legs, neck and chest. She's just getting to her shoulders when Manuel stands up and offers to do her back. She turns to face the sea, offering up her shoulder blades. He rubs his hands slowly over her skin. His movements are confident, emphatic, like he wants to make sure she grasps the full measure of his sensuality. He applies the cream like he's exploring uncharted territory—a woman's back, her flesh, her heat—like it's his raw desire for her that he's spreading on her skin. She lets him caress her back. Her body shifts, almost imperceptibly, a few millimetres in Manuel's direction, the slightest cant. She lets herself slide, be drawn into his chest, without crossing the line into impropriety. She doesn't give in completely. She stays focused on the horizon, on the line not to be crossed, but the attraction is there, and growing by the minute, crackling along invisible wires stretched out between them, it seems, fine and charged with electricity, implanted in each one of their pores. She's surprised to realize that she wants more of this man; she could simply give in, just lean back against his chest, turn her head and kiss him. But she resists, possessed of the realization that he makes her want to tear down the walls she's erected between herself and all men since leaving Jean.

He's awakened the most vital, deepest part of her, she's amazed and delighted to discover, although just at the moment she's fixated on the feel of his hands. He rubs the lotion into every inch of exposed skin on her shoulders, down the length of her spine, in the small folds on the sides of her breasts and waist, as far down as the inverted triangle of the bikini bottom covering her buttocks. He lingers over all the dips and hollows of her back. It draws them closer. She surrenders to the feeling, her head growing heavy. He's confident, but not cocky. It's not yet a foregone conclusion.

Before leaving the beach, in the late afternoon, they drink giant mojitos at Manuel's favourite *chiringuito*. The waitress seems to know him well and goes heavy on the rum. Back at the apartment, they end up stretched out together on Claire's bed, discussing the poems of García Lorca, which Manuel had left lying on the sheets for her that morning.

"You're serious? You want to read me poetry?"

Claire bursts out laughing, and it's the first time he's seen her let go like that. Claire, so uptight, so serious since their visit to the museum, launches herself backwards on the bed like a little girl, arms flung open, legs relaxed. She makes a circling motion with her index finger next to her temple, above her bright smile, made even more dazzling by the effects of the rum cocktails imbibed in the sun.

The smell of salt rises off their damp skin, wafting through the closed air of the bedroom. They stay like that for a minute, lying on their backs watching the ceiling fan turn. Then, in a decisive move, Claire slides closer to Manuel, a sideways scoot, a shifting of the hips, and lays her head on his chest. He's surprised, happy; he begins to stroke her body with his fingertips. He grazes her skin softly, proceeding with caution, waiting to see how things will play out.

He doesn't have to wait very long. Claire raises her head and presses her lips against his as though it were the most natural thing in the world. They kiss hungrily, and it's not long before their bodies meld into one another. Manuel trails his fingers delicately over Claire's hip bones, his hand lingering gently on her belly. In a faltering move at once endearing and deliberate, he inches his hand toward the lace edge of her panties, fumbling with one finger, then two, finally fording the elastic waistband with impatience, thrusting his fingers forward, delving into the smattering of hair. His hand cups her mound, his fingers melting into the warm folds of her sex, which grows wetter as Claire runs her tongue over his chest, sinks her teeth into his shoulder, neck, lips. Their plans for the evening—and for the next few days—have just taken an interesting turn.

The shower stall is tiny, with rounded plastic walls and worn nonslip seashell treads surrounding the drain. It's a drab beige but gleaming, and everything is spotlessly clean, albeit outdated. It's the type of shower you'd picture a grandmother gingerly stepping into, closing the door carefully behind her, then struggling to reach everywhere and wash herself, bumping into the walls and barely keeping her balance, and when the soap finally slips between her fingers, it's game over. Impossible for an old bird like her to bend down in such a tight space.

That doesn't stop them from stepping into it together, after making love well into the evening, taking turns bringing each other to climax, then coming together. Their bodies had been drawn to one another, sliding into an easy rhythm. Then they'd started over again, losing all track of time, eventually drifting off between two embraces. Outside, the sky had turned from bright to faded blue to dusky pink, but inside the room, they'd ceased to notice the movement of the clock, the waning of the day. They fell asleep holding hands, after straightening the sweat-soaked sheet under their languorous bodies. Hunger pangs had woken them up.

Claire shrieks and huddles into Manuel's chest, shivering, as he turns the water on with an icy blast. He tells her he likes his showers cold, that it's good for the skin, for the heart. His erection slaps against Claire's behind, rubs against the backs of her thighs, then her stomach when she turns to face him so he can lather her up. She yelps again when he aims the frigid stream at her head, her scalp tingling under the cold water, which runs down her neck and shoulders, stiffening her nipples into hard points.

When he slides his fingers inside her, she decides she doesn't mind the cold water lashing her skin after all. He whispers in her ear that she's very, very dirty and needs to be scrubbed everywhere, all over. His tone is babying, like he's talking to a little girl, but his touch is shameless, his hand penetrating her with brazen eagerness. He pins her against the shower wall, blocking her escape from the cold, cutting jet that he aims directly at her. She gives herself up completely, wracked with spasms and shivers, her body undone by the ecstasy and the cold. The water offers her a form of violent redemption, and her brain swims with a series of bizarre images as her excitement mounts uncontrollably. When she finally comes, she could swear her body has dissolved into liquid, merging with the rivulets forming at their feet and flowing away through the small holes in the drain.

It's Manuel who finally turns off the shower. Without missing a beat, he dries Claire off, with the same nonchalance, the same verve as he would himself. He lifts her arms to get to her armpits; he dries her bottom, the insides of her thighs, her neck and the fold of skin under her earlobes. Claire can feel his excitement pressed against her backside, sliding down her legs as he bends over to dry her feet and ankles, his desire seeming to know no bounds. Still trembling from her pleasuring in the shower, she finds herself wanting more. Manuel doesn't need any coaxing. In one swift motion, he lifts her up and splays her across his hips, her legs dangling on either side. Claire wraps them around Manuel's waist, nuzzles her face into his neck, crushes her breasts against his slick chest. She lets herself be carried, amazed he has enough strength to support the full weight of her body hanging off him like that. He takes a few staggering steps toward the bedroom, but they don't make it that far. He pinions Claire, hair still dripping wet, against the floral wallpaper in the hallway. The water streams down her back, forming a wet spot around the daisies and buttercups as Manuel thrusts into her, legs firmly planted, holding nothing back.

Claire feels the powerful ripples rising inside her, like waves swelling inside the cavity that once housed living beings. Inside her abdomen, her uterus quivers, draws inward and upward, and contracts like a heart muscle as the pleasure surges through her body.

———

They leave the apartment to pick up wine, bread, some fruit. The elevator ascends slowly toward them. It's one of those old-fashioned cage types with the cables, pulleys and brakes all exposed. At each floor, it gives a little jolt, like a mark or a notch that Claire registers curiously in her still-tingling body.

A mother and daughter step into the elevator on the fourth floor. Manuel looks at Claire, and they smile at each other, as much as to say: We reek of sex.

———

They spend the night the same way as the evening, making love.

Claire hooks her legs over Manuel's shoulders, his body looming over hers, and their voices merge into one, out of control, the room filling with pleasure, sweat spraying off them, their two bodies pounding, probing, pressing, clutching at one another, hair, skin, lips and tongues, flesh, hips urging each other to climax after climax, moans, a long cry, high-pitched squeals, then deep groans, whispers and sighs, they give themselves to each other without shame or reservation. They have only a few hours in this lifetime to revel in the desire that binds them.

And when the frenzy finally subsides, Claire lies dazed and sated against Manuel's sweaty chest, their bodies slumped together in the dip in the mattress. She thinks about the irascible old lady next door, who's no doubt been awakened by their cries and the banging of the headboard: old, dark wood against the faded stucco wall. The entire room feels like it's vibrating: walls, furniture, bodies, curtains, window, shutters, all the way down to the stifling air in the courtyard, which fills with pleasure, fierce, potent and unrepressed.

In the dankness of the room, Claire surrenders herself to Manuel's touch, as he trails his fingers idly over her neck, through her hair, gently, trustingly, as one would stroke the back of a small, docile animal or the downy head of an infant. He runs his hand down the length of her spine to the dimples in her lower back, follows the lines of her body, lingers on the curve of her buttocks, then travels back up again; he explores her with his palm, traces her with his fingernails, so thoroughly that her skin comes out in white lines, like a network of chalk trails against the semi-darkness.

Lying on her side, her body pressed against his, she rests an ear against his bare chest, and it's her own heart that Claire hears beating, like in an echo chamber. With each pulse, a realization emerges, trite and terrifying, rousing her from her stupor: It's been a long time since she's felt so oddly alive and peaceful. Claire wonders if it wasn't this deep-seated sense of calm that she came looking for in Valencia.

KILOMETRE 38

... I'm slowing down, I don't know how to keep moving forward, four kilometres, twenty-odd minutes, now's not the time to throw in the towel, keep going, stay on pace, five minutes forty seconds per kilometre, pump your arms, pump your arms, pump them! Go on, catch up to that girl, right there, in front of you...

Run, go on, run like a free woman, Laure!

KILOMETRE 39

... I'm losing all sense of distance, time, I don't know how many more minutes to go, I can't give up so close to the finish line, my legs hurt, everything hurts, I'm thirsty, I'm burning up from the soles of my feet to the top of my scorching head, a vein throbs in the hollow of my neck, I can't take it anymore...

THE SEA AT NIGHT

It's their last night together. Claire is due to catch the 10 a.m. train to Madrid, where she'll connect with her flight home. Manuel has made her saffron rice with chicken, peas, sliced onion. But the pan is getting cold on the stove. His guest is late and not answering his text messages. He's starting to get worried.

Earlier that day, after dropping his car off with the mechanic, he'd wandered aimlessly around Valencia, checking his phone obsessively, waiting for her at a café, hoping to spot her on one of the boulevards, desperate for any kind of reassurance: She mustn't have checked her phone, must've thought his trip to the garage would take longer. She must be out exploring Valencia, taking her time.

Claire had got lost trying to find the sea. She'd walked for ages, initially in the wrong direction. Then she'd caught a bus without thinking to ask where it was going. She'd walked some more, her skin turning redder by the hour. She hadn't eaten and surprisingly wasn't very hungry. She felt abstract, like one of those heroines in a movie or a novel who wanders through the city streets with her face shuttered, indifferent to virtually everything. Why go looking for the beach? She was in no mood for sunbathing. She'd be all alone there. Still, she wanted to see the place again because her only memory of it was a dull, grey seascape shrouded in fog.

Eventually, she'd found a tram stop. She'd followed the crowd of young girls, ponytails swaying, tanned skin glowing, beach bags slung over their shoulders. She'd boarded behind them without buying a ticket, gotten off at the same station. Then she'd kept walking, a ways away from the sea, in front of the cafés and shops, casting a sideways glance at the long expanse of sand. This is what she'd come here to see: the long shot. She didn't care about the waves, the water, the bodies stretched out on towels, the sand. All she wanted was a horizon, a tableau of vanishing points, a mental postcard of the beach in Valencia. In the distance, parasols. Around the edges, tacky souvenir stands. The beach a nondescript rectangle of sand.

The hours tick by with no news from Claire. Manuel doesn't understand why she's running away from him like this. He'd have liked to spend as much time as possible with her before she left, to have her in his sights, in his arms. He wants her. He can't stop pacing. He wishes the door would swing open, now, right this minute, and she'd walk through it wearing that dress that hugs all her curves; he would nip at her shoulders, nuzzle her neck, get reacquainted with the sweet wetness between her legs. He's starting to feel possessive about a woman he'll never see again.

Claire gets back around 6 p.m. She's shocked that he's waited for her this whole time.

"I'm sweaty and I'm exhausted," she protests, as he wraps an arm around her waist to pull her close.

"I was worried about you," he murmurs into her hair.

Jerking free of his embrace, she says, "Don't worry about me, ever. Alright, I need to cool off. I'm going back downstairs for a quick dip."

Manuel would like to keep her from leaving, but he doesn't know how. Her aloofness throws him off. He'd have liked to go with her, but he's too absorbed in his own sulking.

"Don't be long," he says. "I want to take you to watch the sunset at that place in the marsh where they rent the rowboats."

He steps out onto the balcony to watch her as she wades into the sea. Her shoulders are hunched as the waves break around her waist. Her back is magnificent, and even at this distance the urge to wrap his arms around her is visceral.

Claire returns, smiling and refreshed, her hair dripping. She pulls off her bikini top, and her pert, pink nipples, hard and puckered, spring up to greet Manuel.

Now that she's naked, she's another woman entirely walking around the apartment, liberated, vibrant.

"Not to rush you, but we'll need to leave soon if we want to get there in time to rent a rowboat."

She looks at him, unsure.

"Do you think I could run there?"

She'd like to get a run in before dark. She's doing her best to follow her training program to the letter and not skip any of her five weekly runs. She throws on a pair of shorts and a tank top, slathers sunscreen on her face, arms and legs already burnt from her day of walking. She straps on her watch, and they walk together to the bus stop. Manuel doesn't want to drive because he thinks it'll be hard to find parking. The sunset, like all sunsets everywhere in the world, attracts its fair share of tourists.

She kisses him quickly—¡ *Hasta pronto* !—and starts running. After a few steps, she turns to wave at him, and his face lights up with a huge smile. He finds her beautiful—and fast.

She runs in a straight line, past marshlands and dense thickets swarming with insects and shadows; she can hear rustling in the grass, birds chirping in the underbrush. Nature has a soothing effect on her. She realizes she's starting to get sick of this Manuel guy who's clinging to her constantly like a desperate man. The odd car drives by; between each one, she has the road to herself. She lets the scenery wash over her: the smell of the flowers, the sounds of the insects, the suffocating heat of the fading day.

200

At one point, the bus overtakes her. She raises a hand to Manuel, even though she can't make him out; she knows he's inside, among the faces looking out the window. She pumps her arms harder, partly to speed up, partly to show off. He'll wait for her next to the dock. She likes the thought of being alone on this quiet road.

The distance from the big city, the traffic, the crowds of people finally give her a sense of space, some momentum. The untamed landscape is a perfect reflection of her state of mind, of her heart, beating quicker in the late-afternoon humidity, temples pounding, scalp tingling, mind wandering, focused on the physical effort.

She pushes her earbuds back in, turns up the volume.

And I'm falling, and I'm falling, and I'm falling
I am free, I am free, I am free
And I'm falling, and I'm falling
I am free and I'm falling

By the time she meets up with Manuel on the dock, it's too late. The sky is turning an ever-deepening shade of red. Men are busy stowing away the rowboats. They've missed the last departure. Manuel is disappointed; he sulks while Claire sits on the edge of the dock, chest heaving, heart pounding, legs dangling, face streaming with sweat, gazing at the distant point on the horizon where the sun will soon disappear from sight.

———

They take the bus back to the apartment, saying little. Manuel is still annoyed they missed out on the rowboat ride, and Claire tells him again that she really doesn't care, that the sunset was just as spectacular from the dock. The tension eases slightly as they sit down to eat the chicken and rice. They tuck in on the balcony, in the glow of the candles Manuel has lit. Claire compliments him on the meal, on his choice of wine. For dessert, she settles herself in his lap. He lifts her skirt and slips off her panties.

Down below, the beach is cloaked in darkness. Off to the left, a giant screen is showing an animated movie. Families have come out in droves, setting up chairs and beach mats on the sand. Speakers emit a cacophony of explosions and ear-splitting car chases, followed by chirpy tunes. The background noise drowns out their moaning as Claire, straddling Manuel's hips, rubs herself up against him, slides him slowly inside her with a tilt of her hips, hands gripping the metal chair for support.

They make their way to the bed. For their last night together, they have no intention of sleeping. They'll spend it exploring each others' bodies, again and again, allowing themselves a few moments' rest, curled up together in a numb half-sleep.

Claire gets dressed, steps out onto the balcony. She gazes at the sky, almost as black as oil, the waves and the spume, the wet sand. After a while, Manuel joins her. An expanse of pale thigh slips between two balusters as Manuel buries his nose in her neck, inhales. Claire shivers. She looks down. Six floors. Ceramic tiles, illuminated by the fluorescent light in the lobby, like bright, shiny candies at her feet. She clings to the railing. Her upper body leans over it, tipped forward by Manuel, who wraps his arms around her. He's rubbing himself between her legs, back and forth, like a knife on a whetting stone. Claire bends forward slightly at the hips, and her head starts to swim. She can't feel her legs anymore, the attraction of the void is making her dizzy, and all the while Manuel keeps thrusting.

KILOMETRE 40

... I'm running, running, running, everything is starting to sound muffled, and my mouth is so dry, I'm dying for a drink, my thoughts are becoming tangled, like they're stuck to fly paper, everything feels gelatinous, like I'm running through cotton, dazzling white, I keep moving forward, a blind gust of air, a moulted skin on the pavement, I'm shedding the thing that's weighing me down, leaving behind everything that's holding me back, running, running, running, I take a deep breath, surge forward, kneecaps on fire, with each step I drag myself forward, a warm space opens up before me...

LEAVING VALENCIA

The sea at dawn is calm. Like metal, smooth and gleaming, Claire thinks, casting one last look at the horizon in El Perelló. Manuel, his expression serious, loads Claire's suitcase into his car. They drive in silence, then have a farewell coffee together on the patio at the train station restaurant.

At the last minute, he adjusts his glasses, presses his cheek against Claire's and takes a photo of the two of them. Claire gives him a quick peck on the lips. Then she pushes through the turnstile and walks toward the platform without looking back. She boards the train. Her phone vibrates. It's Manuel. He will have found the tote bag on the floor of the backseat of his Mercedes.

Claire stands on tiptoe to stow her rolling suitcase in the overhead rack, slips into the window seat, leans her head back on the headrest. She glances at the dozens of tracks lined up in rows on the other side of the glass, intersecting on the ground, forming vanishing lines overhung by taut cables orchestrating the departures, arrivals, transfers of thousands of passengers each day. She sighs. "It's a beat-up old purse with nothing important in it," she texts Manuel. "Keep it to remember me by."

— ⁓ —

Claire Halde leaves Valencia without knowing if she'll ever be back. It's an unyielding city, one she has a hard time getting her bearings in, with a layout that belies its seaside location. Twice now she's been to Valencia in August, and twice the city's been operating in slow motion, vaguely empty, lethargic. She hadn't come to splash around in the sea or to loll about in the sun. Her memory will be one of blistering, suffocating heat, and two torrid nights with a man she had no intention of falling for, spent exorcizing—through her spasms, her moans, her sighs, and all the sweat and bodily fluids that had seeped from her pores, orifices, mouth, vagina, anus, saliva, mucous, tears—that business of the woman in Valencia. In the shadow of the city where she let a woman die, she had finally felt alive again.

More than any other place in the world, she had managed to lose herself in this city. Even as the train pulls out of the station, she has no concept of north or south, no idea in what direction Barcelona or Madrid, Asia or America lies.

KILOMETRE 41

... one kilometre to go, I'm almost there, one kilometre to go, the crowd is cheering, I can't make out the faces, my head is pounding, I'm disoriented, but I'm still going, I'm somewhere else, over there up ahead, I'm going to make it, I feel an incredible force rising up inside me, I'm not giving up now, I'm so close, my whole body has kicked into overdrive, powering beyond fatigue now, I speed up, I'm giving myself the shake...

LEAVING

At Atocha station, in Madrid, Claire watches the stream of travellers make their way toward the C1 line to the airport. She's incapable of entering the current; she's rooted in place, upright in the passageway, leg glued to the suitcase resting at her feet. She's in the way, forcing people to go around her, annoyed. Claire is struck with a realization: She doesn't want to go home. She rummages around in her bag and pulls out her plane ticket, stares it as though expecting some revelation to flow from it. After a moment, she tosses it on the tracks, on impulse, a visceral motion that comes out of nowhere and lands her in front of the departures board, next to the indoor garden brimming with lush plants growing and blooming under the glass-and-steel dome. There's a train leaving for Seville in thirty-two minutes. She'll go back to Andalusia. After that, who knows, maybe somewhere else, in search of her youth.

The train picks up speed, hurtling away from Madrid at two hundred and fifty kilometres an hour, skirting a pine forest for the first stretch. Before long, it cuts across a field of sunflowers at the foot of a mountain range whose name Claire doesn't know. Two hundred and sixty kilometres an hour. The scenery flashing by holds absolutely nothing of interest. Forehead pressed against the glass, Claire Halde notes with indifference the barrenness of the landscape, nothing more.

42.2 KILOMETRES

... I can see it, I can finally see it, the finish line, I push even harder, I don't hear the cheers, I'm floating, forward, everything is white, the buildings like bones, steel as white as aspirin, that thing I'm longing for with my entire body, the end of the marathon, I feel like I'm passing everyone ahead of me as I round the Príncipe Felipe Science Museum, a giant whale skeleton emerging from the water, still a few metres to go, the water in the ponds is a bright blue, like an inverted sky, my veins course with pure adrenaline, a potentially lethal dose for a weaker heart, a geyser bubbling up, an ocean of ice dissolving, I can no longer hold back this sudden flood, no, I am this sudden flood, my thighs are screaming in agony like my muscles might tear with every step, I speed up some more, nothing is going to stop me...

Run! Go on, faster, my love!

... come, Mama, take my arm, pull me into your slipstream so we can go even faster...

... still a few more seconds to go, pump the arms, lift the knees, go, go, go, faster...

Run! Go on, faster, my love! Faster!

... take my hand, we'll cross the finish line hand in hand, Mama, like that time in the Caribbean, with the turtles, I can see you next to me, suspended in your ray of light, I squeeze so hard I can feel your bones in my moist palm, I can hear the tide breaking at our backs, I close my eyes, another wave lifts us, we cover the last few metres without touching the ground, with oceanic ease, we float together upright...

Raise your arms, Laure, be proud of yourself, raise your arms above your head, you're a marathoner!

... a remarkable stillness, for a second my body is no longer in pain, I'm nothing but joy and exhaustion. I am a marathoner.

I look at the screen on my wrist: three hours fifty-nine minutes and thirty-seven seconds.

The euphoria and fatigue send me reeling. The dam in my head finally bursts. Without warning, my muscles are wracked with spasms, my chest heaves, struggling to contain my racing heart. A warm breeze blows over my skin, caressing the sweat on the surface, teasing the damp hairs at the back of my neck. Someone hands me a bottle of water. A medal is placed around my neck. I run my tongue over my dry, salty lips, my face finally relaxes, my hips throb, and I smile like I've never smiled before. I limp toward the Assut de l'Or Bridge, which stands out starkly against the blue of the sky. Some people think it looks like a harp, like the Samuel Beckett Bridge in Dublin, others a ham holder. I see a ship, a sailboat ready

211

to cast off. As I draw closer to its white steel mainsail, with its almost translucent shrouds, my pride swells to fabulous proportions. Shivering, I wrap myself in a foil blanket, which I clutch tightly against my body, like an embrace that I vanish into altogether.

QC FICTION

Visit **qcfiction.com** for details and to subscribe
to a full season of QC Fiction titles.

Printed by Imprimerie Gauvin
Gatineau, Québec